**'But tell me th[...]
do you hate mo[...]**

Jordan continued, 'Me for showing you what you're capable of feeling? Or yourself because for those few minutes you acted like a real woman, not a scared little girl!'

Jordan let her go, his gaze contemptuous as he strode back up the path. Katherine watched him go with tears burning in her eyes. She wanted to scream after him that it wasn't true, but he wouldn't believe her. Why should he? Both of them knew what had happened that night. One year later she was still paying the price for it.

Jennifer Taylor was born in Liverpool, England, and still lives in the north-west, several miles outside the city. Books have always been a passion of hers, so it seemed natural to choose a career in librarianship, a wise decision as the library was where she met her husband, Bill. Twenty years and two children later, they are still happily married, with the added bonus that she has discovered how challenging and enjoyable writing romantic fiction can be!

Recent titles by the same author:

RACHEL'S BABY

WIFE FOR REAL

BY
JENNIFER TAYLOR

MILLS & BOON®

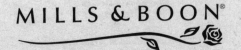

First published in Great Britain 1997
Harlequin Mills & Boon Limited,
Eton House, 18-24 Paradise Road, Richmond, Surrey TW9 1SR

© Jennifer Taylor 1997

ISBN 0 263 80542 5

Set in Times Roman 10½ on 11½ pt.
02-9801-54139 C1

Printed and bound in Great Britain
by Mackays of Chatham PLC, Chatham

CHAPTER ONE

KATHERINE felt the ripple of excitement which ran around the church as another guest arrived for the wedding. It had to be someone really special, she mused, to have caused such a stir. She turned to see who it was but one of the ushers was blocking her view of the newcomer.

She turned back, and smiled as she caught her brother's eye. Peter gave her a brief smile in return, then looked away almost immediately. He seemed lost in a world of his own as he sat with his head bowed and his fingers worrying the carnation pinned to his lapel.

Katherine frowned, wondering not for the first time what was wrong. It was normal for the groom to be a little nervous on his wedding day, but even last night, when they'd had dinner together, Peter had appeared unusually tense. He had eaten only a few mouthfuls of the meal she had prepared for them, but had drunk rather too much of the wine which had accompanied it.

Katherine had been tempted to say something about that. But she had consoled herself with the thought that Peter would have drunk far more if he had gone out with his friends for a stag night party. She had been delighted when he had asked if he could spend the evening before the wedding with her, yet now it struck her as an odd thing to have done. Was there something wrong? Something that Peter hadn't told her...?

'Katherine.'

She recognized the deep voice at once and her heart

seemed to stop beating as she turned to look at the tall, dark-haired man standing beside the pew. 'Jordan... what...what are you doing here?'

'Where else would I be on such a special occasion?' He smiled cynically as he slid into the seat beside her. 'I'm sure people would start wondering what was wrong if I didn't turn up for your brother's wedding, and that's the last thing we want, isn't it? So let's set everyone's mind at rest straight away.'

Before Katherine could guess what he intended, he leant over and brushed her mouth with a kiss. His lips were cool, despite the heat of the June day. They sent a tingle, almost like a shiver, racing through her. Katherine jerked her head away, her grey eyes darkening in shock as they met the mocking blue ones which were staring at her.

'Smile, darling. Everyone's watching.' Jordan laughed softly, so softly that Katherine knew she was the only one to hear the taunt in his voice. 'I'm sure they're all delighted to see husband and wife having such a touching reunion—today of all days.'

Katherine drew back abruptly. She could feel the shock rippling through her; frissons of alarm were mixed with other feelings she didn't want to think about too hard right then. 'I...I had no idea that you were coming. Charles never mentioned that you would be back in time for the wedding.'

'Didn't he? But then Charles only manages the firm in my absence. He isn't my confessor. I don't report everything I intend to do to him.' Jordan smiled, but his eyes were hard. 'You've seen him recently, then, I take it?'

Katherine nodded, wondering why she felt so uncomfortable. It was the way Jordan was looking at her, his expression almost accusing, although she had no idea what she was being accused of.

'I saw Charles on Thursday night, as it happens. He'd managed to get tickets for the final performance by the Russian Ballet. It was kind of him to invite me to go with him.'

Her grey eyes challenged him to disagree but Jordan merely shrugged. 'Very kind. But then that's the sort of man Charles is—kind and considerate. Nothing at all like the man you married, Katherine.' He gave a deep laugh as he saw her colour rise at the mocking comment. 'Still, Charles does lack my one real virtue. He doesn't have my money, does he? What a pity. He could be perfect apart from that rather large flaw.'

Jordan picked up the service sheet and started to read through the list of hymns. Katherine took a small breath but it didn't help. She could feel herself trembling, and hated the feeling that she wasn't in control. It was all due to the strange way Jordan was acting—that plus his unexpected arrival, of course.

She frowned, wondering why he had turned up like this. He had always been meticulous about letting her know if he would be attending any function they had been invited to. So why hadn't he done so this time? After all, it was a system which had worked well over the past year. Appearing together on the odd occasion kept up the front that their marriage wasn't the sham they knew it to be.

Jordan had made it plain when she had told him that she could never live with him that he didn't want anyone to know the truth. Katherine had been happy to agree to his demands because they suited her as well.

It had proved surprisingly easy to convince everyone that their marriage was a success simply by attending a few engagements together. Jordan was out of the country on business so often that they had the perfect excuse to keep those occasions to the minimum—no more than three or four in the past year, in fact. Whenever they met, he treated her with a cool courtesy which had soon quietened any fears she'd had as far as his motives were concerned.

They lived virtually separate lives beyond that. When he was in London, Jordan either slept at his club or Katherine went to stay with her father so that he could use the flat in Mayfair. He travelled extensively, overseeing the latest projects his company was working on, so that sometimes Katherine found herself wondering how much time they would have spent together anyway, even if they hadn't come to this arrangement.

Business came first with Jordan, and nothing was allowed to get in the way of it—especially not any unsavoury gossip as to the state of their marriage. But surely it would make more sense in the not-too-distant future for Jordan to rid himself of a wife who didn't fulfil his needs, and find another who did?

Katherine gave a small, bitter smile as she glanced at him. But then why would he choose to go to all that trouble when there must be many women eager to supply everything he wanted without him making such a commitment? Jordan could easily have his cake and eat it. Katherine was certain that he did!

He must have sensed her watching him because he suddenly turned. His eyes darkened as they rested on her delicate face in its frame of soft blonde hair. The expression in them was hard to define.

'Mmm, one might almost think that you missed me, Katherine. Did you? After all, it's been…what…almost two months since we saw one another last?' He laughed huskily. 'They say that absence makes the heart grow fonder, don't they?'

'So I believe. However, like most maxims, there is always another to contradict it.' She gave a sharp laugh and felt her heart beat a little faster as she heard how false it sounded; she wondered if Jordan had heard its falseness too. Try as she might she could never be truly indifferent to him. There was just something about him which got under her skin no matter how hard she fought not to let it affect her. 'Out of sight, out of mind seems appropriate in this case.'

She looked away, yet she couldn't deny that she felt shaken by what he had said. Why on earth should he imagine that she missed him? The more distance there was between them the better, as far as she was concerned, and she would have thought he felt that way as well.

The organist suddenly struck up the bridal march to announce the arrival of the bride. Katherine stood up with the rest of the congregation. Her arm brushed Jordan's and she drew away at once, but it would be impossible to avoid touching him.

The tiny village church was packed with guests and there was little room to move—far too little to avoid making repeated contact. Yet each time it happened Katherine felt another jolt of awareness run through her, so that by the time the ceremony was over her nerves were in shreds. Maybe it was that which made her over-react when Jordan took her arm as they followed the bride and groom down the aisle.

'Let me go!' Katherine dragged her arm out of his grasp as she glared up at him with stormy grey eyes.

'Surely you're going to forgive me darling?' Jordan smiled, but his eyes were glacial as he took her arm again and held it firmly. 'I did try to get here sooner but it was one delay after another. Flying back from Tokyo is a *little* more difficult than getting here from Mayfair!'

Katherine heard someone behind them laugh in appreciation of Jordan's wit. She only wished she could share their amusement. However, another glance at Jordan's face warned her that it would be a mistake to cause a scene.

In silence she let him lead her from the church, waiting until they were well away from the rest of the guests who were milling around as the photographer tried to organise them into groups. Only then did she wrench her arm free again, making no attempt to hide her displeasure.

'Oh, dear, something does seem to have upset you. I suppose you'd better tell me what it is and get it over with.' Jordan raised a lazy brow, although his face was hard behind the smiling mask. In the sunlight she could see silver streaks in the dark hair at his temples and the tracing of fine lines which netted his eyes at the corners.

Jordan would be forty in a year or so's time. He had lived his life on the edge for so long that the years had left their mark on him, even though they hadn't softened his attitude. What Jordan James wanted he got; what he didn't like he discarded. Katherine wondered slightly hysterically which category she fell into.

'You know perfectly well what's wrong!' she retorted sharply, stung by the thought.

'Even if I weren't too damned tired to play guessing games, this is neither the time nor the place for them.' He glanced over her shoulder, his eyes narrowing as he watched the crowd moving about. 'We'll be wanted in a moment, so if there's something you want to say then let's hear it, Katherine. I don't want you creating scenes all day long because you're spoiling for a fight.'

His words took her breath away, and it took a few moments before she could speak. When she did her tone was like cut glass, each word sharp and clear, so that there would be no danger of him misunderstanding. 'I'm not spoiling for a fight, Jordan. I'm not interested enough to argue over something as trivial as your sorry lack of manners!'

'Indeed?' He gave a soft laugh as he leant back against the trunk of a spreading oak tree. Sunlight filtered through its leaves, dappling his face with shadows, making it suddenly hard for Katherine to see his expression clearly. 'So it's my lack of manners which is bothering you, is it? I'm afraid you're going to have to explain that, as I have no idea what you mean.'

She drew herself up, feeling suddenly uneasy. What was it about the way Jordan was acting which made her feel as though boundaries which had been set a long time ago had been crossed? She tried to shake off the feeling but it stayed at the back of her mind, unsettling and disturbing.

'It's quite simple. I had no idea that you would be here today. I thought that you were still involved in negotiations for the new contract with the Japanese. Quite apart from the fact that Charles never mentioned you were coming home, I spoke to your secretary only a couple of days ago and that's what she told me.'

'And she was right. I had no idea I would be able to get back in time for the wedding until yesterday, and even then it was touch and go in case something went wrong. The Japanese struck a hard bargain, but in the end we managed to come to an agreement which suits us both.'

Katherine didn't doubt that. Nor did she doubt that the contract Jordan had secured would be a lucrative one. His business acumen was legendary, his hard-headed approach earning respect and fear from allies and competitors alike.

J.J. Engineering had won contracts for an impressive list of civil-engineering projects worldwide in the past few years. The Japanese contract would be yet another guarantee that the firm would earn more kudos. It wasn't what interested Katherine, however.

'I see. However, hearing that you were still tied up, I naturally assumed that you would be unable to attend the wedding. I informed Mr and Mrs Hartley accordingly and offered your apologies. Turning up like this without warning is inconsiderate in the extreme, Jordan.'

'Oh, dear, is that what's bothering you? The table plan? Now I understand. You must forgive me, Katherine, but I hadn't given any thought to that. How could I have been so lacking in the social graces? It's a good job I have you around to put me straight whenever necessary, isn't it?'

Katherine's face flamed at his sarcasm. She swung round, refusing to remain there and allow him to mock her. However, before she had managed to take even a step, Jordan caught hold of her wrist and stopped her.

He swung her back to face him, his eyes devoid of any trace of amusement as he stared into her angry face. 'Don't lie, Katherine. If nothing else, at least do me the courtesy of telling me the truth. You don't give a damn about upsetting Mr and Mrs Hartley's arrangements, do you? It's the fact that I turned up here without warning you beforehand that's eating you, isn't it?'

He slid his hand beneath her chin, forcing her face up to meet his contemptuous stare. 'What's the matter, my sweet? Afraid that I might want to take a few more liberties now that I've overstepped the mark this far? Worried that I might be growing tired of this marriage of ours and thinking about changing the rules? And who could blame me?'

He stared at her for one long moment more before abruptly letting her go. 'I believe we're wanted. I suggest we leave this discussion until later. I'm sure neither of us wants to spoil your brother's big day.'

He walked away, not bothering to look back to see if she was following as he joined the other guests. Katherine watched him pass some comment, heard the laughter which ran around the group. Jordan had charm by the bucketful when he chose to use it, but it left her cold...

She ran a hand over her hair to smooth the silky waves back from her face. She could feel her hand trembling but wouldn't allow herself to think of the reason why—apart from the fact that she loathed any kind of a scene. She smoothed her jacket down too, the lace rippling beneath her fingers. She had chosen the outfit because it was her favourite colour—pale cream, cool and elegant.

She always dressed in understated colours—cream and beige, navy and black. Her hand hesitated on the expensive cloth as she suddenly wondered why.

Did she wear them as some sort of disguise, so that she could hide from the world? Wasn't it her biggest fear that one day someone would guess that behind the cool façade another woman existed? No one had ever suspected it apart from her. It had lain hidden, dormant, until that night when Jordan had shown her exactly what she was. The shame was something she would have to live with all her life. The only way of coping with it was never to allow it to happen again.

Katherine took a slow breath and then made her way over to the group. She stood beside Jordan as the photographs were taken, and played her part, smiling for the camera, looking pleased that she was there to witness her brother's wedding. She didn't allow herself to think about her own wedding just one year earlier, let alone remember what had happened on her wedding night...

CHAPTER TWO

'IF YOU'LL excuse me, I'll just go and phone my father to let him know how everything went. Unfortunately, he hasn't been well recently and the journey here would have been too much for him today.'

'Give Adam my regards, Katherine, and tell him I'll speak to him soon. But hurry back, darling. It's been far too long since we had any real time together!'

Katherine saw the indulgent glances everyone exchanged and she avoided looking at Jordan as she made her way from the huge marquee which had been set up in the grounds of the Hartleys' house, and took the path leading down the garden. Telephoning her father had been just an excuse to get away.

She followed the path until it reached the fence which marked the boundary of the property. Resting her arms along the rough wooden bars, she stared towards the distant hills while she tried to get a grip on herself, but it wasn't easy.

The day had been a nightmare; the effort involved in playing her part had left her drained. Jordan had kept her at his side all afternoon while they had chatted to the other guests. He had been as urbane as ever, yet whenever she had glanced at him he had been watching her with an expression in his eyes which made her feel shaky even now, when she remembered it.

What did Jordan want with her? It was a question she had asked herself a dozen times yet she still didn't know the answer. She just kept remembering what he had said in the churchyard earlier, about sticking to his side of their bargain.

Had it been said in anger to scare her? Or had there been a deeper intent behind those harshly spoken words? She had no idea, but the uncertainty made her feel sick with fear. She could cope with this marriage but only so long as Jordan didn't try to make any changes!

A twig suddenly snapped and Katherine swung round, her heart turning over at the thought that Jordan might have followed her. She needed a few minutes by herself to get her emotions under control, although she wasn't sure that it would be possible even then.

The way Jordan had been acting today seemed to have unleashed a whole torrent of fears so that she felt raw and exposed, as though a defensive layer had been peeled away to leave her more vulnerable than she had felt since the night of their wedding. When Peter suddenly appeared out of the trees, she gave a little gasp of relief.

'Oh, it's you!'

Peter paused when he saw her, then slowly walked over to join her. 'Sorry, I didn't mean to scare you. What are you doing here, anyway?'

'I...I just felt like a breath of air,' she hedged. 'It's very hot in the marquee, but everyone seems to be having a wonderful time.'

'Yes. Diane's parents have spared no expense in giving her a day to remember. Although perhaps she'll prefer not to have any reminders of what a mistake she's made!'

'What on earth do you mean?' Katherine felt her heart lurch as she heard the anguished note in her brother's voice.

'Nothing. Forget it.' Peter turned to stare towards the

hills, but not before she caught the glimmer of tears in his eyes.

She touched his arm in concern. 'Obviously something is wrong, Peter. I had a feeling about it earlier, to tell the truth.' She glanced round and frowned. 'Where is Diane? Surely you two haven't quarrelled, have you?'

Peter shook his head. 'No, of course not. Diane's in the house getting changed. We'll be leaving shortly to catch our plane.' He gave a harsh laugh. 'The way I feel, I wish we were never coming back!'

'Peter!' Katherine stared at him in horror, more concerned than ever as she saw the strain etched into his thin face. 'Please tell me what's wrong and if there is anything I can do to help.'

'There's nothing you can do, Kitty.' He gave another of those bitter laughs which were so out of character. 'There's nothing anyone can do!'

'I don't believe that.' Katherine took a quick little breath to control the growing feeling of panic. 'There is always a solution to every problem. It's just finding it that is difficult sometimes. Tell me what's wrong, Peter, then maybe we can work something out together.'

'Like we did when we were kids? After Mother left, it was always you I ran to to solve my problems, wasn't it? But somehow I don't think you can help me this time—not unless you happen to have a spare fifty thousand pounds lying around.'

'Fifty thousand pounds?' Katherine repeated numbly. 'Why on earth do you need so much money? It's a fortune!'

'Don't I know it? And I have as much chance of getting my hands on that kind of cash as I have of flying to the moon.' He ran his hand over his eyes. 'It will mean the end of Diane and me once she finds out, of course. She'll never forgive me and neither will her parents. And I love her so much, Kitty! I really do. If only there was a way—'

He stopped abruptly, and when he turned Katherine could see a glitter in his eyes which alarmed her even more.

'Peter, what is it...?'

His hands clamped on her shoulders so that she winced. 'Jordan! I should have thought of him before. Will you ask him, Kitty? Ask him to lend me the money? I swear I'll pay him back somehow.'

Katherine shook her head, stunned by the request. 'No...I couldn't possibly. I mean, I don't even know what you need it for!'

'Because I'm a bloody fool, that's why! I let a couple of the fellows I work with talk me into going to this gaming club with them. It was all just a bit of fun at first. I even won a couple of times. Diane was furious when I let slip what I'd been doing. She made me promise never to go again.'

'But you did go?' Katherine guessed. 'And this time you lost? Oh, Peter, how could you be so stupid?'

'I know. I know! I just kept telling myself that the next time I would win, but it never happened. Now the people I owe the money to are threatening to go to Diane's parents. They've given me two weeks to come up with the cash. Two bloody weeks!' Peter gripped Katherine even harder. 'Jordan's my only hope! Please, *please*, say that you'll ask him, Kitty!'

'I don't know... I don't know what to say...' Katherine felt a lump in her throat as she saw despair settle over Peter's face as he let her go.

'I understand. I should never have asked you to do it. I...I'd better get back and see...'

She couldn't stand it. She couldn't bear to see him looking so dejected. 'All right, then, I'll ask Jordan.'

'You will?' Peter gave a whoop of joy as he swung her off her feet. 'Oh, you don't know what a weight that is off my mind!'

'He hasn't agreed yet,' Katherine warned him.

'But he will if you ask him!' Peter gave her a quick hug. 'I'd better get back to Diane before she thinks I've run out on her. You will ask him as soon as you can, though, Kitty, won't you? I don't want those people running to Diane's parents and causing a fuss while we're away.'

Katherine opened her mouth to repeat her warning that she wasn't sure if Jordan would agree, only Peter was already hurrying away. She shivered as she turned to stare towards the shadowy hills again. The thought of asking Jordan for all that money scared her, but what else could—?

'Well, what are you waiting for, Katherine? They always say there's no time like the present, so why don't you get it over with right now and ask me if I'm willing to lend you fifty thousand pounds for Peter. Or are you waiting to catch me at the right moment?'

Jordan gave a soft laugh which made her skin prickle as she turned and saw him standing in the shadow of the trees. 'Mmm, I'm almost tempted to find out exactly when that is.'

Katherine took a deep breath and tried to close her mind to the nuances she'd heard in his voice, but she could feel ripples of awareness spreading through her, as though he had touched one nerve and all the others were responding.

'I...I didn't know you were there,' she said huskily.

'No? Never mind; don't let that deter you.' He gave

another of those disturbing laughs as he came and leant against the fence beside her. He was so close now that she could smell the musky aroma of the aftershave he wore, and she could feel the heat of his body flowing through the thin fabric of her jacket. Suddenly it was as though all her senses were heightened to an almost unbearable degree, so that when his shoulder brushed hers she jumped, and saw the amused look he gave her.

'Nervous, Katherine? I don't see why you should be. After all it isn't the first time you've found yourself thrust in at the deep end to help a member of your family out of a sticky situation, is it?'

Katherine's face flamed as she understood what he meant immediately. It had been the need to help her father out of even worse financial straits that had brought her and Jordan together—although if she'd had any idea of the repercussions she would never have gone through with it!

She turned to glare at him, her grey eyes stormy as they met his mocking blue ones. 'No, it isn't new to me, Jordan. However, that doesn't mean I find it any easier second time around.' She gave a harsh laugh. 'In fact, bearing in mind what happened the last time I asked you for help, I must have been mad to let Peter talk me into asking you again!'

Jordan's lids flickered but his smile never wavered. 'You got what you wanted, Katherine. Your father has been able to live comfortably ever since. Are you really trying to claim that you would have preferred to see him being dragged through the courts and ending up with nothing more than his name at the end of it?

'No! Of course I wouldn't have wanted that to happen. You know very well what I mean, Jordan!'

'Of course I do. How could I be in any doubt,

Katherine?' His brows rose, his eyes glittering as they centred on her angry face. 'You have always been totally honest about your feelings towards me, haven't you?'.

Katherine looked away, wondering what there was in the depths of his eyes which made her feel as though she was standing on the edge of some vast precipice, and that one unwary step would send her plunging into its unknown depths. 'I...I don't think either of us is under any illusion about how we feel. However, that has little bearing on this present situation.'

'Hasn't it?' Jordan's tone was openly sceptical, the mockery she heard in it making her heart beat even faster.

'No.' Katherine's hands clenched as she turned and stared into the distance while she fought to keep all trace of emotion from her voice. 'Will you lend Peter the money he needs? That's all I want to know.'

'I'm sure it is, but has it never occurred to you that every time you bail Peter out it just makes matters worse? He is old enough to stand on his own two feet, but he'll never do that while you keep fighting his battles for him.'

Jordan's tone was scornful, and Katherine reacted immediately to it despite her determination to remain detached. 'That's not fair! How on earth can Peter get himself out of this mess?'

'Not as easily as he apparently got himself into it, *Kitty*.'

Jordan mocked her with the childhood name, yet it was a measure of how upset her brother had been that he should have used it tonight. The thought made her even angrier. Jordan considered himself so infallible that he couldn't understand how anyone else could make a mistake!

'Unfortunately, not everyone is as perfect as you, Jordan! But surely even you could see how upset Peter was? Is it too much to ask that you try to be a little more sympathetic?'

He smiled contemptuously. 'I imagine that Peter is far more interested in the support I can give him financially rather than emotionally. I shall leave that side of it to you.' He sighed, sounding suddenly weary. 'However, this is hardly the place to discuss Peter's failings. I came to tell you that it's almost time for him and Diane to leave; so shall we get back to the party? We can sort this out later.'

'No. We need to sort it out now. I want to be able to tell Peter if you're going to help him or not. Jordan, wait!'

Katherine felt her temper rise to dizzying heights as Jordan started to walk away. She caught hold of his arm to stop him, determined that he was going to give her an answer. It was only when she felt him go utterly still that she realised what she had done.

She never touched him—not willingly, at least. In the whole year of their marriage not once had she reached out and placed her hand on his arm as she had done just now. Now the shock of the contact spread through her so that her fingers and arm tingled.

There was a moment's tense silence before Katherine abruptly let him go. She drew a ragged breath of air into her deprived lungs while she avoided looking at him. But she sensed that Jordan was watching her. It disturbed her to wonder what she would see in those deep blue eyes if she looked...

'It's still there, isn't it, Katherine?' His voice was so low that it barely disturbed the silence of the night, yet she still jumped. Her eyes flew to his face, and what she saw there filled her with fear. Jordan was looking at her with an assurance and a certainty which allowed no room for doubts as he continued in that same soft tone.

'Despite how much you hate yourself for it, you still feel that same desire for me that you felt on our wedding night.'

'No!' Katherine felt the blood drain from her head so fast that she thought she was going to faint. 'You're wrong...wrong! I don't feel anything for you, Jordan. Do you hear me? Nothing at all except...except contempt!'

She tried to push past him, her whole body trembling with the shock of what he had just said. Jordan caught her wrist, his fingers cool and hard as they closed around her flesh to hold her still.

'Don't lie, Katherine! We both know what the truth is. Do you think I'm stupid? Do you imagine that I don't know how you felt on our wedding night?'

'Yes. You must be stupid, or incredibly arrogant!' She gave a sharp laugh, then bit her lip as she realised she was verging on hysteria. She forced herself to meet his eyes, wanting desperately to convince him that he was wrong. 'I know it comes as a shock to you, Jordan, but not every woman falls under your spell. If you want the truth, I hated what happened that night.'

His hands tightened; the violence she sensed in him made her wonder if she had pushed him too far. Then suddenly he gave a deep laugh, mocking, taunting, knowing...so very knowing, which was so much worse.

'Mmm, is that a fact? You're sickened by the idea of me making love to you? All you felt that night was revulsion? Is that what you're saying, Katherine?'

'Yes! What does it take to convince you? Is your ego so huge that you can't accept that I'm telling the truth?

I hated you touching me, Jordan. I hated the thought of you anywhere near me!'

'Like you're hating me touching you now? Is that why your heart is racing, Katherine?' He pressed his finger to the pulse which was throbbing at the base of her neck, and let it rest there, so that Katherine could feel its warmth branding her flesh. She jerked back, struggling to free herself, but Jordan was too strong for her to break the hold he had on her.

'Let me go, Jordan.'

She saw his smile deepen. When he let his finger slide up her neck to come to rest by the corner of her mouth she closed her eyes, terrified of what he might see in them right now—all the turmoil and anguish she felt, all the shame that even now his touch could have such an effect on her.

'It wasn't loathing you felt that night, Katherine. Oh, you might have fought me like a she-cat, but it wasn't because you were disgusted by what was happening— far from it.' He slid that tantalising finger beneath her chin, forcing her head up. 'You wanted me, Katherine. You wanted me with a passion that you had never ex-pected, didn't you? After all, you hadn't married me because you were in love with me, so how could you have suspected that you would feel like that?'

His voice was like a drug, soft and deep, and so com-pelling that her eyes opened almost of their own volition. Katherine stared into his face, seeing the truth of what had happened that night—which she had tried so hard to escape from.

'No. Jordan, I...'

He didn't seem to hear her as he continued, in that same quiet tone which made a mockery of her halting attempts to deny what he was saying. 'Maybe I was wrong to do what I did, but it wasn't planned. It just happened, and for those first few minutes when I took you in my arms you responded to me. You can lie to yourself but we both know I'm right.

'But tell me this, my sweet, who do you hate most? Me for showing you what you're capable of feeling? Or yourself because for those few minutes you acted like a real woman, not a scared little girl!'

He let her go, his gaze contemptuous as he strode back up the path.

Katherine watched him go with tears burning in her eyes. She wanted to scream after him that it wasn't true, but he wouldn't believe her. Why should he? Both of them knew what had happened that night. One year later she was still paying the price for it.

No matter how hard she tried she could never forget how she had lain in Jordan's arms and felt for him a passion she never wanted to feel again!

CHAPTER THREE

It was almost three a.m. when Katherine heard the sound of a key in the lock. She hadn't gone to bed. There had been no point—she had known she wouldn't be able to sleep.

Jordan had left the reception shortly after Peter and Diane had left for their honeymoon. Katherine wasn't sure where he had gone but she suspected that it might have something to do with Peter.

She had stayed up, waiting for him to return, longing for him to get back but also dreading it. Of course she wanted to know that Peter had nothing more to worry about, but it was the price Jordan might demand in return for his help which worried her. She knew to her cost the kind of bargain Jordan struck!

He was in the hall taking off his jacket when she opened the sitting-room door. He glanced round, and Katherine realised how exhausted he looked. There were deep lines etched either side of his mouth and his skin looked grey beneath its tan.

'I thought you would be in bed by now.' He tossed his jacket onto a hook then leant against the wall as though he was almost too tired to stand up. 'Should I be touched that you waited up for me?'

The fleeting concern Katherine had felt disappeared at once. She stared coldly back at him, hating the way he kept taunting her like that. It was something he had never done before; it made her wonder a little fearfully what had changed to make him do so now. 'I assumed that your absence had something to do with Peter's problems. I wanted to know what had gone on and if you had decided to help him.'

'Of course.' Jordan gave a soft laugh which held just a thread of menace. His eyes were cold as he came along the hall, the tiredness in them not quite hiding his contempt. 'I should have realised that any concern you felt was purely on behalf of your beloved brother. Silly of me to imagine anything else, wasn't it? I must be more tired than I realised.'

Katherine swung round, refusing to stand there and debate the point when her nerves were already so on edge. 'I'll make some coffee. You look as though you could do with some.'

'Mmm, there's a lot of things I could do with, my sweet wife, but I doubt I'm going to get them tonight.'

There was a nuance in his voice which brought the colour to her face. Katherine busied herself filling the percolator until she was sure that the colour had faded. Yet, when she glanced round, Jordan was watching her with an expression in his eyes which made her realise he had seen her reaction. The thought unsettled her even more, so that her hands shook and the coffee scattered all over the worktop.

'Leave it. Instant will do. I'm too tired to wait around for that to be ready, anyway.'

He sat down at the table and closed his eyes as he ran his hand around the back of his neck to ease the aching muscles. Katherine watched him for a second, then hurriedly switched on the kettle and made two mugs of instant coffee. She set them on the table and sat down opposite him.

'God, what a day!' Jordan sighed as he opened his eyes and took a sip of the hot liquid. 'I don't remember

ever being this tired before. Must be jet lag, I suppose.'
He looked up and smiled sardonically. 'But I don't expect you're interested in hearing about my problems, are
you, Katherine? I imagine you're waiting to hear if Peter
is off the hook.'

Katherine ignored his sarcasm. 'And is he?'

Jordan laughed, but it wasn't a pleasant sound. 'That's
what I admire about you. You go straight to the important things in your life, and there is nothing quite so
important as your brother—oh, and your father, of
course. We mustn't forget him, must we? Not when he
was instrumental in bringing us together in the first
place. Don't you feel just the tiniest bit aggrieved with
your father for that? Or do you prefer to blame me for
this predicament you find yourself in? Married to a man
you loathe.'

'I have no intention of sitting here listening to this!'
Katherine went to get up, shaken by what he had said.
It just confirmed all her fears that something *had*
changed. They'd had a tacit agreement not to mention
the past, but today Jordan seemed to be taking every
opportunity to rake it up. However, with a speed which
shocked her, he reached over and caught her hand.

'Don't run away. I am merely stating a fact, not trying
to start an argument again if that's what you're worried
about. The only reason you married me, Katherine, was
because I had it in my power to save your father from
bankruptcy. Neither of us is under any illusion about
that.'

He gave her a brooding little smile as his fingers slid
up her arm beneath the sleeve of her jacket. They felt
cool against her skin and she shivered involuntarily, but
Jordan didn't appear to notice. She was grateful for that,
because she felt vulnerable enough without him making

anything out of the fact that she trembled when he touched her!

'I wonder if it would have turned out better if I had been more like the men in your circle, the men who play by the rules you understand—like Charles, for instance. You and Charles seem to get on very well, but then you have so much in common, don't you?'

'I cannot see any point in this conversation. How well Charles and I get on has no bearing on this at all!' she retorted, stung by the way she was reacting to Jordan's touch.

'Hasn't it?' Something crossed his face, an expression which made Katherine's breath catch when she saw it. She must be mistaken, she thought wildly, because there was no reason for the sudden rage she could see in his eyes.

'You've been seeing a lot of Charles recently, haven't you, Katherine? The ballet the other day, probably the opera or an art exhibition as well. Unfortunately, I know very little about such things. But then you and Charles come from very similar backgrounds—a world away from how I was brought up, believe me.'

'I…I really do not see where this is leading, Jordan. My friendship with Charles is neither here nor there!'

She tried to draw her hand away, but Jordan's fingers tightened and he gave a harsh laugh. 'So that's what you and Charles are—friends? I see.'

'What do you mean? What do you see? Exactly what are you implying, Jordan?' Katherine felt her heart leap as she heard the scorn in his voice.

'Why should I be implying anything?' His eyes were suddenly hooded as they rested on her angry face. 'I was merely trying to determine if our marriage could have been a success if I were like the other men you know, but I don't suppose it would have made a scrap of difference.

'The last thing you wanted from me or any man was a real relationship, wasn't it? You were simply willing to trade yourself in exchange for what I could do for your father. Now we shall have to see what you are prepared to do to help your brother.'

'I imagine it depends on what you ask in return for helping Peter, doesn't it?' She gave a bitter laugh, anger washing through her in red-hot waves to chase away the nervousness she felt. How dared Jordan speak to her like that?

'If we are establishing facts then let's get them straight. If I was prepared to trade then so were you! Or are you trying to claim that you fell in love with me, and that's why you wanted to marry me? I don't think so!'

She dragged her hand free, barely noticing the way his eyes flickered behind his heavy lids. She had no idea why he was acting like this, but if he imagined she was going to sit there and take whatever he cared to dole out then he was mistaken!

'You wanted a suitable wife who knew how to entertain your clients and I wanted to help my father. Those are the facts. They have nothing to do with Charles or anyone else. It was just that you, with your usual arrogance, decided to change the rules! Our marriage could have been perfectly amicable if you hadn't taken it upon yourself to show me things you thought I should know!'

She pushed back the chair so that its legs scraped against the tiles. The noise was harsh and discordant. Katherine's nerves strained at it. She felt incredibly angry. How Jordan felt she had no idea. He was just sitting there staring down at the mug of coffee, his head bowed almost in defeat…

That thought fled from her mind as fast as it had appeared. She had to bite her lip to stop herself from laughing hysterically. 'Defeat' wasn't a word Jordan understood!

'So, are you going to tell me where you went tonight and what happened, or not?'

There was a moment when she thought he wasn't going to answer, and then he looked up. There was no anger on his face, nothing to show how much he resented the things she had said, but that didn't fool her. Jordan must be furious about the way she had spoken to him. Her heart lurched as she wondered if it had been wise in the circumstances.

'Why not? After all, you more than anyone are entitled to know what your brother has been up to, Katherine.'

There was something in his voice, an undercurrent, which made her skin prickle with apprehension. Katherine drew a ragged breath as she recalled what he had said about how far she would be prepared to go to help Peter…

'Then you had better tell me exactly what you found out, hadn't you?' She forced down the fear and struggled to appear composed, but it wasn't easy. Jordan had more reason than ever to extract a high price for his help!

He smiled narrowly as he picked up his cup. 'It appears that your brother doesn't owe fifty thousand pounds after all.'

Katherine blinked in confusion. 'But why did he say that he did? I don't understand.'

Jordan slammed the cup down so hard that she jumped. 'It's simple. Peter owes closer to one hundred thousand. The fifty grand he needs so urgently is just the start. It just so happens that the owners of one particular club have decided to call in his debt, and I'm sure the rest of his creditors won't be far behind them once word gets out. From what I was able to discover, Peter owes various sums to at least half a dozen clubs around London.'

'No!' Katherine gripped the table as the room swam out of focus. 'Are…are you sure? It could be some sort of a silly mix-up—even…even a deliberate attempt to extort money. I mean, who's to say if those people didn't just tell you that in the hope that you would settle the debt for Peter?'

'I don't think so. They wouldn't be that foolish!' Jordan's laughter was harsh, brutal even. In the bright overhead light his face looked tough and uncompromising, with a cold cynicism glittering in his eyes which made her shiver as she saw it.

She knew his reputation, of course. Jordan was a tough negotiator and few who crossed him survived to tell the tale. There had been many articles in the papers about the way he had fought his way to the top with a ruthless determination. He never compromised, never accepted second best, never allowed anything to deter him from his goals. If anyone could help Peter out of this situation then it was Jordan, but what he would expect in return remained to be seen!

She took a quick little breath to control the rush of fear as Jordan continued in the same uncompromising tone. 'It appears that an attempt was made to contact me once it was realised how deeply in debt your brother was getting. Unfortunately I was out of the country at the time, so the message never reached me.'

Katherine frowned in bewilderment. 'I don't understand. Why should these people have contacted you?'

'Because your brother gave my name as a reference when he asked to extend his credit. Somehow it was allowed to slip through without a proper check being done, and once one club had agreed to the new credit limits the others followed suit. Alarm bells only started ringing when people realised that he was in way over his head, but by then it was too late.

'Unless Peter finds a way to repay the money he'll be ruined. There is no way that he'll be kept on at the Stock Exchange once word gets out, and believe me it won't take long before that happens.'

'No!' Katherine stared at Jordan in despair. 'Is…is there anything we can do?'

'That depends.' Jordan looked down at the mug. When he looked up again, Katherine could see something in his eyes which made her heart beat so fast that she could feel the blood swirling through her veins.

'On what?' Her voice was whispery-thin in the silence. She licked her parched lips and made herself repeat the question she didn't want to ask. 'What does it depend on, Jordan? What are you saying?'

'That it is up to you what happens, Katherine. Peter's future depends on what you decide to do.'

'I don't understand…'

'It's simple.' Jordan leant back in the chair as he watched her through narrowed eyes. 'I am willing to pay everything Peter owes and write off the money so that he doesn't need to repay me a penny of it. However, there are certain conditions attached to my offer…naturally.'

He made it sound like some sort of business proposition. Katherine wished she could believe it was that simple! Her mind ran wild trying to understand, but she had no idea what he was proposing—that was the trouble. 'And those conditions are…?'

'That Peter gets the help he needs to stop gambling. I also expect him to give me a written undertaking, enforceable in a court of law, that he will never use my name again without my permission.'

'That seems fair.' Katherine managed a shaky smile. As far as she was concerned Jordan was being more than charitable in the circumstances.

'That isn't all, Katherine. There is one other condition attached to my offer. One which concerns you. I want you to think very carefully before you decide, because once you do there will be no going back on your decision. You have to be sure that you can carry it through if you agree to my terms.'

Katherine's fingers were numb because she was gripping the table so hard. As though from a distance she heard her own voice, thin and shallow, asking the question, 'And that condition is?'

'That we end this sham of a marriage.'

The blood rushed through every bit of her so fast that her fingers tingled and her body throbbed. It was relief, she told herself, the sheer relief of hearing those words that was causing this reaction. To imagine that there was the slightest trace of disappointment at it was ridiculous.

'Of course. I shall give you a divorce any time you—'

Jordan's laughter was so harsh that she flinched. 'Oh, no, Katherine, that isn't what I want! I'm sorry, I must have phrased it badly. Put it down to tiredness or whatever.'

He gave her a slow smile, his blue eyes playing over her white face. 'In fact, what I want is just the opposite of what you imagined. I want to end the sham of the way we live by making our marriage a real one in every sense. I want us to live together properly as man and wife, to share a roof and a bed. And what I want most of all, Katherine, is a child.'

'A child?' She could hear the shock echoing in her voice, feel it rippling through her in waves. She stared at Jordan in disbelief, wondering wildly if she had misheard him. 'You…you want us to have a child?'

'Yes.'

'I…I don't know what to say. I never imagined…' Katherine swallowed hard but her voice was still strained. 'Why do you want a child, Jordan?'

He gave a wry laugh. 'For all the usual reasons, I imagine! I'm no different from any other man in wanting a child to carry on my name and inherit all I have worked so hard to achieve.'

'But why now, so suddenly, out of the blue like this…?' She tailed off, unable to continue, unable to absorb what he was telling her and to make sense of it.

'But it isn't out of the blue. I've been thinking about this for some time.' He met her eyes levelly. 'I'm not getting any younger and I would like to have a child before I'm too old to do all the things a father should do with his son or daughter. But what about you, Katherine? Surely you want to have children while you're still young enough to enjoy them?'

'I…I never thought about it,' she whispered hollowly.

'Because you're married to me?'

'What do you mean?' She stared at him in confusion as she heard the sudden bitterness in his voice.

'Simply that you had put off thinking about having a family because of the implications.' He shrugged, but his gaze was dark and intent. 'It would entail sleeping with me, wouldn't it, Katherine? And we both know how you feel about that!'

Her face flamed with angry colour and she stared back at him with stormy grey eyes. 'Yes, we both know how I feel about that, Jordan. At least there's no confusion on that score. It's a pity that you aren't as clear in your own mind about what you want and why.'

His brows rose, but he seemed more amused by her outburst than anything else. 'Meaning what, precisely?'

'That a child isn't something you can bargain with like…like a clause in a contract! A child should be loved and wanted for the right reasons, not because it's something you need to perpetuate your name!'

'Oh, I agree, Katherine. I am in complete accord with you on that. It seems that you do have some views on children after all—even though you may not have thought about having a family yourself. Maybe you should do so now.'

He got up from the table. 'In fact, that is what I want you to do—to think about what I have said very carefully before you tell me what your answer is. I'm afraid I shall have to stay here for the night as it's too late to go to my club. We can talk about it again in the morning.'

He turned to leave, but Katherine couldn't let him go like that. 'You can't really expect me to agree to such a proposal? It's insane!'

He glanced back, his eyes shadowed by his lowered lids. She felt a frisson run down her spine as though he had physically touched her. 'It isn't insane at all. We're married, Katherine. We can either accept that and try to make the best of it or we can carry on the way we are. Are you really happy with your life as it is at present?'

'But why do you imagine that a child would make it

better? It wouldn't alter the reason we married, Jordan. It wouldn't change that! Nothing can.'

She gave a shrill laugh. She could hardly believe they were having this conversation. A child! She couldn't begin to think of what it would mean, how it would change her life. It would be the ultimate tie, of course, because she could never leave Jordan if they had a child...

Unlike her mother, a voice inside her whispered. Her mother had found it easy to leave her children because she'd had other needs. What if she was like that? What if she turned out to be like her mother in that respect as well...?

Katherine's hands clenched as she tried desperately to hold onto her control, but it seemed to be slipping further and further away with each second that passed. 'It's out of the question,' she said hoarsely. 'There is no way that I shall agree!'

'I don't want you to give me your answer right away.' He held his hand up when she started to speak. 'No. This is too important an issue to make some hasty decision about. You need to think about it first.'

'There is nothing to think about!'

'Maybe you feel like that now because it's been a shock.' He shrugged, with an oddly tender smile playing about his mouth which startled her. 'But once you think it through you may change your mind. You have a lot of love to give, Katherine. I know that from seeing how you behave towards your father and brother. A child would benefit from all that you have to give it, because you would make a wonderful mother.'

He left the room, and after a few moments Katherine heard the door to the spare bedroom closing. She sank down onto a chair, trembling in the aftermath of what Jordan had said.

A real marriage.

A marriage where she and Jordan would live together day by day, sleep together in the same bed, share all the intimacies of man and wife.

And a child. Jordan's child...

She bit her lip as fear rushed through her in a great wave. The problem was that Jordan had no idea what he was really asking of her, but then how could he have? It was something she had never discussed with anyone; she was too ashamed to admit her secret fears.

How many times as she'd been growing up had she heard the comment passed about how like her mother she was? It had been meant as a compliment, because Caroline Carstairs had been a beautiful woman.

After Caroline had left, however, the comments had stopped abruptly. No one had wanted to point out the resemblance then, but the damage had been done. Katherine had been tormented by the thought that she might be like her mother in other ways, and all it had needed were those few minutes in Jordan's arms to confirm her worst fears.

How could she allow that to happen again when the memory filled her with such shame?

She closed her eyes as the wave of fear engulfed her and she was drawn down into its dark depths. Yet how could she refuse and watch her brother's life being ruined?

CHAPTER FOUR

SUNLIGHT poured through the window and touched Katherine's face. She stirred. It took her a few seconds to realise that she was lying on her bed fully clothed, a few more before she remembered why...

She struggled to her feet, shocked to see that it was midday. She couldn't believe that she had slept so late, even though it had been dawn before she'd crept into bed, exhausted by the effort of going over and over everything that had happened...

She felt a wave of panic wash over her as all the fears of the previous night compounded, but she made herself take a deep breath. She and Jordan had been too keyed-up last night to talk rationally, but surely today would be different? If she could convince him that his demands went way beyond what was reasonable then maybe they could come to some amicable arrangement. After all, it wasn't inconceivable that Peter might be able to repay the money Jordan lent him, if he was given enough time.

Katherine clung to that thought as she went to find him, but there was no sign of Jordan in either the sitting-room or kitchen. She glanced along the hall, wondering if he had gone out without waking her, then frowned as she saw that the guest-room door was firmly closed. Had Jordan overslept as well?

He was lying sprawled face-down on the bed when she eased the door open to peer into the room. He was still wearing his shirt and trousers although he had kicked

39

off his shoes. He must have been exhausted to have slept so long, Katherine thought. But then he'd had that flight to contend with as well as everything else.

She was just debating whether she should wake him when he rolled over onto his back and started muttering a little. Even from where she stood, Katherine could see the hectic flush on his cheekbones, the beads of perspiration glistening on his brow. She frowned in sudden concern, wondering what was wrong with him.

The heat was what she noticed first as she hurried to the bed and bent down to look at him. It radiated from him as though his whole body were burning up. Tentatively she laid her hand on his forehead, and was shocked to feel just how hot he was. She was just trying to decide what she should do when his eyes suddenly opened to stare straight into hers.

'Katherine…'

His voice was husky as he said her name in a way he had never said it before. Katherine felt the tiny hairs all over her body stand up as though he had actually touched her. She jerked her hand away and saw the shutters come down over his eyes as he suddenly returned to full consciousness.

He eased himself up on his elbow, then groaned. 'God, my head hurts! What the hell's the matter with me? I can't remember having much to drink yesterday.'

'You didn't. From the look of you you're running a temperature, I'd guess. Do you want me to call the doctor?' She forced herself to speak calmly but she could hear the tightness in her voice. It was the way that Jordan had said her name just now, his voice throbbing with something, which sent ripples of sensation running through her as she remembered it.

He shook his head, then groaned again since that had

obviously made it ache even more. 'There's no need. A couple of aspirin and I'll be right as rain.' He looked up and smiled tauntingly. 'Sorry, Katherine, but I doubt that I'm going to make you a rich widow yet awhile, if that's what you're hoping for.'

She drew back, deeply affronted by his mockery. 'I'll get you those aspirin. I won't be a minute.'

'There's no rush. I think I'll just have a shower first. It will make me feel better, I hope!'

He swung his legs over the side of the bed and struggled to his feet. Katherine debated the wisdom of what he was doing before she decided it wasn't any of her business. She hurried back to her own room to shower, then dressed quickly in jeans and a black T-shirt before going to the kitchen.

She filled a glass with water, then took the aspirin out of the cupboard and loosened the childproof cap. Of course she would have to make sure that any medicines were kept well out of reach if there was to be a child running about...

The thought slid into her mind so fast that she had no warning before it was there. She closed her eyes as she strove to shut it out, but it simply grew stronger, took on shape and substance. Suddenly she could picture a small boy with Jordan's black hair and blue eyes laughing up at her...

Her hand shook as she picked up the glass and chased away the moment of foolishness. There would be no child! She would find some way to convince Jordan that the idea was crazy just as soon as he was in a fit state to listen to her.

Jordan was still in the shower when Katherine went back to his room. She set the glass and bottle of aspirin down on the bedside table, then went to the bathroom door. 'I've brought you the aspirin. They're beside the bed.'

There was no answer, although she had raised her voice to carry over the sound of the water. Katherine felt suddenly uneasy as she remembered how unsteady Jordan had looked when he had got out of bed. Like it or not, she couldn't just walk away without checking if he was all right.

She opened the bathroom door, ready to retreat if need be. But one glance at the figure slumped against the tiles confirmed her fears. She ran into the room and crouched down beside him. 'Jordan…are you all right? Can you hear me?'

He seemed to have some difficulty focusing, judging by the way his eyes slid over her face. 'Dizzy,' he muttered thickly. 'Awfully dizzy.'

'Here, let me help you up.' Katherine tried to haul him to his feet but he was a dead weight. She crouched down again, to slide her arm around his waist, trying not to notice the bare contours of his body. But it was impossible not to be aware of the sleek power of the muscles which rippled beneath her fingers, impossible to ignore the warm, male scent of his skin.

It took several attempts before he managed to struggle to his feet, but it was obvious that he wouldn't be able to make it to the bedroom until he had rested. Katherine propped him against the wall, using her weight to counterbalance his.

His skin was still burning hot, despite the shower, and she could feel its heat seeping through her clothes. It disturbed her to realise just how intimately they were standing; her body was pressed against Jordan's naked one from breast to thigh.

She eased back, then had to hurriedly reach out and

steady him as he swayed. Her palms pressed flat against the hard wall of his chest, and the thick whorls of black hair which covered it twined sensuously around her fingers.

Katherine felt her heart lurch as she felt its springiness. She curled her fingers into her palms, to free them from the bondage of hair, and felt her nails rasp down his skin—almost…almost as though she were caressing him…

Unbidden, her eyes lifted, and she felt the blood rush to her face as she saw the gentle amusement in Jordan's heavy blue eyes. 'Mmm, I bet you didn't bargain for this when you offered to help me, did you, Katherine?'

The wryness in his voice made her smile despite the tension which was coiled like a tightly wound spring inside her. She smoothed her hands flat against his chest, trying not to notice how the hair curled around her fingers again, as though intent on holding them there. 'I definitely didn't!'

He gave a throaty laugh as he looped his arm around her shoulders. 'Well, I for one could stay here all day like this, but I don't imagine it would be wise—for any number of reasons. Shall we try and get to the bedroom, sweetheart?'

The tender endearment made her heart turn over. Katherine didn't try to answer because she was afraid of what Jordan might hear in her voice. She slid her arm around his waist as he took a tentative step away from the wall, and felt a rush of alarm as his legs seemed to buckle.

'Careful! Hold onto me, Jordan. Don't let go!'

He drew a deep breath, yet his voice seemed to grate breathlessly. 'That sounds like the best suggestion I've ever heard. Holding onto you is my intention, Katherine.'

Katherine shot him a startled look, but there was nothing on his face to explain her feeling that there had been a double meaning to the words. She concentrated on helping him back to the bed, and was relieved when he finally sank down onto it. Jordan was a big man, tall and well-built, despite the fact that he didn't carry an inch of spare flesh, and if he had passed out then she would have had no hope of moving him.

He lay back against the pillows with a sigh and closed his eyes, his body bathed in sweat and trembling from the exertion. Katherine drew a ragged breath, then bent to lift his legs up onto the bed to make him more comfortable. Even his legs were hot to the touch, the fever obviously raging through every bit of him...

Her gaze skimmed upwards before she realised what she was doing, and she felt her pulse leap. Jordan's legs were long and well-muscled, his calves firm under their heavy coating of black hair, his thighs powerfully contoured, his hips narrow...

Katherine's heart raced so that the blood drummed inside her head. She wasn't a prude, but the reality of looking at a naked man as powerfully built as Jordan was a world removed from studying a painting or a piece of classical sculpture. Jordan's masculinity was raw and potent, and something inside her responded to it despite herself.

She turned away abruptly, aware that she was trembling as she hurried to the wardrobe and found a spare blanket. Her hands were shaking, as though she were the one caught in the throes of the fever, as she carried it back to the bed and spread it over him.

'Don't want...' Jordan stirred as he felt the soft wool envelop him. 'Too hot, Katherine. Take it 'way...'

He tried to push the blanket off, but Katherine caught his hands and held them still. She took a deep breath, deliberately ridding her mind of those dangerous feelings by focusing on making him comfortable. Oddly it was something she *wanted* to do rather than simply feeling she had to.

'No, leave it there. You'll get a chill if you push it off. Just lie still, Jordan, and go to sleep, then you'll feel better. Will you do that for me?'

His lips twisted into a smile as he gazed at her with heavy blue eyes. 'Just for you, Katherine. Only for you...'

His lids lowered and he was asleep in seconds, the raspy sound of his breathing filling the room. Katherine stared down at him, studying the way his thick black lashes lay on his cheeks like two small fans. She felt something inside her stir. Tenderness? Compassion? Neither seemed to be exactly what she felt right then, but then neither seemed to be the sort of thing she usually felt when she thought of Jordan either!

She glanced down, suddenly realising that she was still holding his hands. He had nice hands, she thought as she turned them over. They were strong, capable hands; his fingers were long and beautifully shaped, his nails were cut blunt, and his skin was so darkly tanned that it made a startling contrast to her own...

Katherine felt her senses swim. She closed her eyes, trying desperately to blank out the pictures which suddenly filled her head. She had tried so hard to forget that night, yet suddenly it was as clear as though it were happening all over again: Jordan's hands sliding up her pale, naked body to cup her breasts; the hunger in his eyes as he looked at her; the hot, moist feel of his mouth as it closed over her nipple…

And the clearest, most terrifying memory of all: the way *she* had responded as he had shown her that she was a woman…exactly like her mother!

'Normally I would insist that your husband went to hospital, Mrs James. However, in view of the fact that he is so adamant that he doesn't want to go, and that this isn't the first time he has had malaria, I think it will be safe enough to allow him to remain here.'

'Is there anything else I need to know?' Katherine opened the door as the doctor picked up his bag. 'I'll make sure that he takes the medicine you've prescribed for him, of course.'

'That's the main thing.' The doctor smiled reassuringly as he saw the concern in her eyes. 'Your husband will be fine, Mrs James. It's just a question of letting the illness run its course. There will be bouts of fever followed by periods when he will feel chilled, and he may even appear slightly confused at times. However, just make sure that he's comfortable and he should be right as rain in a day or so.'

'Thank you, Doctor.'

Katherine closed the door, then went back to the bedroom. Jordan was asleep again, lying quietly enough beneath the blanket now. She tried to decide if he looked any better but it was hard to tell. All she could do was wait for the illness to run its course, as the doctor had said, although she still couldn't quite believe what was the matter with Jordan.

Malaria! Never in her wildest moment would she have suspected that was what was wrong. But the doctor had seemed in little doubt after Jordan had explained that he'd had it before. It made her wonder suddenly where he had caught it, but then there were so many things about him which she didn't know. Their marriage hadn't been founded on a mutual need to get to know one another, but on something far more basic. Maybe they had been foolish to imagine that it could have worked in the circumstances.

Katherine moved away from the bed and went to the window to stare out. The evening rush hour was almost over but there was still plenty of traffic moving along the street. Its sound was muted to a low hum which made a background for the thoughts humming inside her head.

Would either of them have gone into this marriage if they'd had any real idea of how it would turn out? She couldn't speak for Jordan, and it was equally difficult to answer the question herself. Even with the benefit of hindsight she had trouble deciding.

She turned to glance at the man lying in the bed and sighed. There was a strange sense of *déjà vu* about everything which had happened in the past two days. Eighteen months ago there had also seemed little alternative but to ask Jordan for help...

When Katherine discovered that her home in Suffolk had been mortgaged to the hilt and that the bank was about to call in its loan, she realised that something had to be done. Carstairs Engineering had been losing money for years, and since her father's heart attack six months previously affairs had gone from bad to worse.

Adam Carstairs was in no state to deal with the problem, so Katherine decided upon a course of action—not even consulting Peter to determine his views. Shielding Peter from any unpleasantness had become a habit by then.

She had met Jordan James several times and hadn't particularly liked him. There was something about him that bothered her, which in itself was a surprise— Katherine preferred to view everyone she met with the same detachment, but she couldn't quite manage to treat Jordan James that way. However, if there was anyone who could help it would be him, so she made an appointment and went to his office.

He listened courteously as she outlined the advantages his firm could expect by buying out Carstairs Engineering. There was a small smile playing around his mouth which worried her just a little. He sat back in his chair as she finished and nodded.

'You put your case extremely well, Katherine.'

'Thank you.' Katherine inclined her head graciously, trying to quell the unease she felt about the way he was looking at her. What was it about the expression in those dark blue eyes which made her feel as though he wasn't surprised by what she had told him? She had no idea, but the thought lingered at the back of her mind.

She took a quick little breath, determined not to let the feeling deter her. 'However, if I have put my case well then it's because there is a very strong case indeed. My father's firm has been established for a great many years and has an enviable list of past clients to its credit. By taking it over, your company would enjoy the benefits of that.'

'Mmm, you are extremely persuasive.' Jordan laughed softly. His eyes were very dark as they rested on her now, the expression in them subtly altered. Katherine had the feeling that he liked what he saw, and she shifted uneasily, although it had never bothered her before when a man had found her attractive.

'However, I must confess that I have done a little

homework already and come up with a few facts which aren't quite as attractive.' Jordan sat forward in his chair, and Katherine felt a frisson run down her spine as she saw that his smile had disappeared and that his face looked suddenly hard and uncompromising.

'Indeed?' She clenched her hands, trying not to show how nervous she felt as she wondered what he meant. Jordan James was a tough negotiator; she knew that much about him even if she knew little else. Her father had made a point of inviting him to dinner over the past few months, which was how she and Jordan had met. In fact, Adam Carstairs had seemed quite keen to encourage a friendship between them, now that she thought about it. It made her feel more uneasy than ever to wonder why.

'Nobody is trying to disguise the fact that the firm has been going through a rough patch recently,' she said cautiously.

Jordan's brows rose. 'Carstairs' is verging on receivership. I would call that rather more than a "rough patch".' He must have seen the start she gave because he smiled sardonically. 'I told you I've been doing my homework, and, from what I have learned, Carstairs' has little to offer apart from a vast amount of debts. As for the benefits of its previous-client list, I'm afraid it takes more than one gentleman's recommendation to another to secure a contract in today's market.'

'I see. Then I really cannot see any point in discussing this further.' Katherine stood up abruptly. She couldn't recall ever having felt this angry. How dared Jordan James sit there and make fun of her? 'I'm sorry I have wasted your time, Mr James—'

'Leave it to me to decide if you are wasting my time.' He didn't allow her to finish. His voice was hard-edged, and Katherine stiffened, sensing immediately that she wasn't going to like what he said.

'It will be simpler if I put my cards on the table, I imagine. Your father has sold or mortgaged everything he owns in the past few years. Your home in Suffolk belongs to the bank, along with the flat in Mayfair and even the cottage in Cornwall. His debts run into millions and he has no hope of paying the money back. The whole lot will go *and* he will be declared bankrupt into the bargain.'

'What are you talking about?' Katherine clutched her bag with hands which had gone ice-cold. 'There is no question of my father going bankrupt!'

'That's where you're wrong. I'm afraid it's simply a matter of time now. His creditors won't wait for ever, take it from me. Is that what you want to happen, Katherine?'

'N…no. Of course not,' she whispered. 'I had no idea things were that bad…'

She took a shallow breath, her head reeling with what he had told her. She had known about the house, of course, but not the rest of it… She looked at him, eyes clouded with despair. 'What can I do? Believe me, I will do anything to save my father from that sort of disgrace. The shock would kill him!'

'There is a way you can help him.' Jordan sat back in his seat, and there seemed to be a brooding quality to the look he gave her now. 'You see, I realised some while back that this situation could arise and made my plans accordingly.'

'Plans? I don't understand.' Katherine stared at him in confusion, then felt her heart lurch as he got up and came around the desk. She looked up at him, her grey eyes huge, the pulse in her throat beating wildly as her heart raced. She saw Jordan's eyes drop to it and, when they rose again, her breath caught at the expression in them...

It was gone so fast that she knew she must have imagined it, because there was no trace of anything on his face now—no sign of that wild desire she thought she'd seen!

Her hands clenched until her nails bit into her palms, but she welcomed the pain, needing it to hold onto her control, which was in danger of being completely eroded. 'I think you had better explain what you mean, Mr James!'

'Of course, and it's quite simple. I am willing to buy out Carstairs' and guarantee that the sum involved will cover all your father's debts. I am also willing to meet his expenses for the next X amount of years. I believe it has been suggested that a spell in a more temperate climate would be beneficial once he leaves hospital? Naturally I would cover all his living and medical expenses.'

'How do you know that?' Katherine demanded hoarsely, stunned by his knowledge of her father's private affairs.

He shrugged lightly, seeming almost amused by the question. 'I made it my business to find out all I could.'

'I see. Well, it seems to me that you have gone to a great deal of trouble, Mr James,' Katherine retorted sharply, stung by his arrogant belief that he had the right to go delving into things which didn't concern him. She could hardly believe that he'd had the nerve to do such a thing, but then it was obvious that Jordan James played by his own rules.

'However, I doubt you're offering to do all this out

of the goodness of your heart, so exactly what do you
want in exchange for your benevolence?'

'You.'

For a moment Katherine thought she must have misheard him, but then he laughed drily. 'No, that's what I
said, Katherine. I want you in exchange for saving your
family from penury. It's that simple.'

'If this is some sort of a joke—' she began hotly.

'It isn't a joke.' Jordan's fingers were firm as he led
her over to some chairs grouped around a coffee table
in the corner of the room. 'Sit down. I'll get you a drink.
You look as though you could do with one.'

He opened a cabinet and took out two brandy glasses,
then poured a little spirit into each. However, when he
tried to hand her one, Katherine shook her head. 'No, I
don't want it. In fact I don't want to stay here a moment
longer and listen to—'

'Sit down, Katherine.' His tone was just sharp enough
to make her obey him. Almost before she realised what
she was doing, she had sat down. He set a glass in front
of her, then sat down in the chair opposite and studied
her quietly.

Katherine stared down at the brandy while she tried
to understand what was going on. It was only too easy.
She had a very good idea of what Jordan James wanted!

'Obviously I didn't make myself clear.' There was
amusement in his eyes when she looked up. 'What I am
offering, Katherine, isn't some seedy little affair.' He
took a sip of his brandy and smiled as though he found
the idea funny.

Katherine picked up her own glass and let a little
brandy burn its way down her throat. It made her feel a
bit better, a bit more in control. 'Then what are you
offering, Mr James?'

'Marriage.' He sat back and sighed. If he heard the small gasp she gave then, he gave no sign. 'I have reached a point in my life when it makes sense to get married, you see. Of necessity I do a great deal of entertaining—clients both from home and abroad. I need someone who understands how to handle that kind of situation, a woman who can smooth over the odd awkward moment with tact and diplomacy.'

'I'm sure there must be any amount of women willing to act as hostess for you!' Katherine retorted with some asperity.

'I shall take that as a compliment. Thank you. And what you say is perfectly correct. I can call upon any number of beautiful women who'd be only too willing to do what I require of them. However, expertise in the bedroom doesn't appear to qualify them for being the kind of woman I need by my side when I'm entertaining, or, indeed, being entertained in a client's home.'

Katherine stared down at her glass, refusing to rise to the provocative comment. She had little interest in the women Jordan James knew, and even less in his sex life. She was starting to get a measure of exactly what he was suggesting, however. And she was no longer shocked.

She understood the kind of marriage he was proposing because she had seen it work. Several of her father's friends had married simply because it had been appropriate for them to do so. In her view, those marriages had a far better chance of surviving than the ones supposedly founded on love, which was simply another name for desire. Once one of the partners outgrew their passion, as they always did, there was little left to hold those marriages together.

It was what had happened to her own parents, and

Katherine had seen at first hand the destruction it caused to people's lives. A marriage of convenience wasn't to be dismissed, although it gave her an odd feeling to wonder what it would be like to be married to a man like Jordan James!

'I see. And you feel that I would fit the bill, so to speak?' she said neutrally, to disguise the sudden qualm she felt.

'Yes, I do.' He seemed amused by her coolness, although his tone was as bland as hers had been. 'From what I know about you, Katherine, you would be perfect for the role I have in mind. I believe you have acted as your father's hostess since your mother left?'

Jordan James seemed to know rather too much about her family, but it didn't seem worth commenting upon it. 'Yes. Daddy has always entertained a lot—until his illness, that is. Naturally, I always made all the arrangements for him.'

'Then I can't say anything more, can I? It would solve both our problems. Your father would have the security he needs more than ever at the moment, and I would have the kind of wife my clients expect. Naturally you would have all the freedom you wished, although I must make it clear that I would expect you to be discreet.'

'Discreet…?' Katherine felt her face heat as she realised what he meant. 'Oh, there would be no need to worry about that, I assure you.' She paused as a thought struck her. She wasn't sure how to phrase it, yet it was a question which had to be asked.

Jordan seemed to guess what was on her mind, however. 'Our marriage could be in name only to begin with, if that is what you would prefer. However, I can see no reason why we shouldn't make a full commitment in time if both of us wanted to.'

Katherine nodded, refusing to think about what it would mean to share the intimacies of marriage with him. It wasn't an issue at present, and if it ever did become one then she would have to think about it…

'So, Katherine, what do you say?'

She felt a ripple run down her spine as he spoke her name. She looked up, her heart beating in an agony of indecision, and felt a sudden fear she barely understood as her eyes rested on him. What was it about this man which bothered her so? That made her more aware of him than she had been of any man? Maybe if she understood that then she could decide what she must do.

'Is it yes or no, Katherine? Make up your mind.'

As he prompted her to answer she felt panic run in icy waves down her spine. 'I…I need a little time. You can't expect me to give you an answer here and now.'

He shrugged, but there was a hard light in his eyes. 'I'm afraid that time is the one thing you don't have. From what I have learned, the bank is ready to start proceedings against your father. We're talking days, here, not weeks.'

'But don't they know he's been ill? Surely that counts for something?' she cried desperately.

'This is business, Katherine.' Jordan smiled thinly. 'Sentiment doesn't enter into it, believe me. And once the bank goes to court it will just make things that much more difficult for your father.'

Katherine got up to walk to the window, her mind racing as she tried to come up with another solution. But there simply wasn't one. Even if by some chance she could find another buyer for Carstairs Engineering there wouldn't be enough money to pay off all her father's massive debts.

But if she agreed to marry Jordan then he would take

care of everything; there would be nothing more to worry about…

She took a deep breath as she turned and held out her hand. 'Then my answer is yes. It…it seems to make a great deal of sense from my point of view as well as yours.'

There was an oddly intent light in Jordan's eyes as he came over to her. He took her hand, but instead of shaking it, as she'd expected, he drew her to him and kissed her cheek.

It was no more than a token gesture, yet Katherine felt a tremor run through her whole body, like the ripples which spread through a pool when a stone is tossed into it. She drew her hand away, her smile stiffly held to disguise how she felt.

'I…I shall leave everything to you to arrange, then, shall I?'

His brows arched, his expression faintly mocking, as though he had sensed her reaction and it amused him. 'Of course. I suggest we set the date for the wedding for six months' time to save any unsavoury speculation. One thing I don't want is for there to be any gossip, Katherine. This arrangement is to remain strictly between ourselves, you understand?'

'Of course. It is what I would prefer too. I don't want my father worrying when there is no need.'

Jordan walked her to the lift and stood there as she stepped inside, that same odd little smile playing about his mouth.

Katherine was left with that picture of him for hours afterwards, and found it deeply unsettling. Had she made a mistake in agreeing to such a plan? It sounded crazy in this day and age. But she knew it could work so long as they both stuck to the rules…

*   *   *

Only Jordan hadn't stuck to the rules, and that was when it had all started to go so terribly wrong...

'Katherine...'

Katherine jolted back to the present as Jordan called her. She took a deep breath, like a swimmer coming up out of the water. For a moment her head swirled as thoughts of that night—her wedding night—rushed back and assailed her, before she managed to push the memories into the darkest recess of her mind.

'Katherine!'

Jordan's voice sounded hoarse as he called her again. Katherine hurried to the bed, yet when she got there his eyes were closed. She shook him gently, then bent closer so that he could see her.

'I'm here, Jordan. Can you hear me? Is there something you want?'

His eyes slowly opened and he stared at her for a long moment. 'Thought you'd gone...left...' His voice faded into silence yet his eyes stayed open, staring into hers.

Katherine felt a shiver dance down her spine at the way he was looking at her. What could she see in the cloudy depths of his eyes that made something deep inside her ache in a response she barely understood?

His lids suddenly dropped, his body twisting beneath the blanket as he began to shiver violently. 'Cold...' he muttered. 'So cold...'

Even as she watched another spasm racked him. Katherine could hear his teeth starting to chatter, yet the room was warm. She hurried to fetch another blanket and tucked it around him, but even then he still kept shivering, drawing his legs up to his chest as he tried to get warm.

He was muttering under his breath now, odd, disjointed words too low for her to catch. Suddenly he thrashed out, kicking the blankets off him, his body shuddering with cold as he lay there. Katherine picked everything up and replaced it, but another violent struggle ensued and the bedding ended up on the floor again.

After half a dozen repeats of this, Katherine was near to despair. If she tucked the blankets tightly under the mattress, Jordan simply struggled even harder, so that several times she feared he would toss himself onto the floor. He desperately needed to be kept warm until the chills passed, but the way he was thrashing about made it impossible to keep him covered.

She took a deep breath as she realised what might help. Lord knew, she had seen it done a dozen times in films, but she had never imagined doing such a thing herself! She slipped out of her jeans, then slid beneath the blankets and drew him to her.

He gave a violent start, his eyes shooting open to stare straight into hers. 'Katherine…?'

Katherine felt the colour run up her cheeks as she heard the shock in his raspy voice. It took every scrap of control she possessed to keep her voice level. 'Shh, it's all right. Just lie still, Jordan, and I'll keep you warm, then you'll feel better.'

He let her draw him to her, his body faintly resistant at first before he gradually relaxed. His head was heavy on her shoulder, and the arm which seemed to loop itself so naturally across her waist pinned her to the bed. Katherine wondered a little wildly if this had been wise, because now she was effectively trapped, yet even as she thought it Jordan settled down. He fell asleep in seconds, his breathing becoming slow and steady, the shivers gradually disappearing.

Katherine stared up at the ceiling, feeling the soft warmth of his breath on her cheek, the weight of his

body pressed all down the length of hers. She took a
deep breath and let it out slowly. It didn't help.

She closed her eyes as she listened to the steady sound
of his breathing, and was suddenly afraid. She might
have married Jordan to save her family but it hadn't been
gratitude she'd felt that night they had almost made love.
She wished it had been, because she could have lived
with that far more easily than the truth.

She had wanted Jordan that night, wanted a man she
barely knew, wanted him with a passion which
had known no bounds... It would be so easy to want
him again!

CHAPTER FIVE

'GOOD morning, Katherine. And how are you today?'

'Fine, thank you, Daddy.'

Katherine had been in the kitchen making coffee when the telephone had rung and she'd hurried to answer it. Jordan was still asleep and she didn't want him to be woken unnecessarily.

She pressed the receiver to her ear, her hand trembling as she recalled the night. She had never expected to fall asleep the way she had. The situation had seemed far too fraught to make that possible. Yet she had woken a little before seven to the realisation that she had spent all night long in Jordan's arms.

Her heart gave a funny little jolt as she remembered how he had looked, lying next to her, his arm still looped across her waist, his face oddly vulnerable...

'Katherine, are you still there?'

She dragged her mind back from thoughts which were far too disturbing as she realised that she'd missed what her father had said. 'Yes, I'm still here.' She glanced at the clock and frowned. 'What is it, Daddy? Why are you phoning so early? There's nothing wrong, is there?'

Adam Carstairs gave a wry laugh. 'It comes to something when my daughter believes that the only reason I phone her is with bad news! But to answer your question, darling, no, there is nothing wrong—at least not with me. I was simply wondering why you hadn't telephoned to tell me all about the wedding.'

'Oh!' Katherine gasped in dismay. 'I'm so sorry,

Daddy! I was going to phone you during the reception but...but something cropped up,' she finished lamely as she recalled why she hadn't made the call. 'I can't believe that I never thought about it since!'

Adam chuckled drily. 'I expect you had other things on your mind. I believe Jordan managed to make it to the wedding after all. Mrs Hartley mentioned it when I phoned her yesterday. No wonder you forgot all about your old father, eh?'

Katherine's face flamed at the gentle teasing. She felt her stomach knot as she wondered what her father would say if he knew the truth. He had no idea that her marriage was a sham... And he would never know! she thought determinedly. It would upset him far too much to find out what she had done and why.

'Yes, he just about made it back in time. I'd had no idea he was going to be there myself until he suddenly arrived at the church, in fact.'

'He promised me that he would try to get there if it was at all possible.'

'Did he?' Katherine frowned in bewilderment. 'What do you mean, Daddy? Jordan promised *you* he'd try to be there? I didn't know that you'd spoken to him.'

She glanced round as she heard footsteps, and felt her pulse leap as she saw Jordan coming into the room. In a fast sweep her widening eyes took in the short black towelling robe he was wearing. He had belted it around his waist but the front gaped open so that she could see his bare chest through the gap, the silky covering of dark hair shadowing it...

Her mouth went dry and she turned away to stare at the wall, trying not to see the picture which was forming in her head—the way that black hair arrowed downwards...

'When I rang him. I was worried about you being there all on your own. I imagine it was a lovely surprise for you, Katherine; it must have made the day even more special having Jordan there.'

She forced herself to concentrate on what her father was saying. 'I…yes, of course. I just wish you'd warned me, though, Daddy.'

She heard the sound of water running and couldn't stop herself from glancing round again. Jordan was at the sink, filling a glass with water. He turned off the tap, then raised the glass to his lips, watching her as he took a long swallow.

Katherine felt her heart turn over as she saw the way his throat moved convulsively while he drank. There was something strangely seductive about watching him perform such a simple act; she found she couldn't look away. She felt her nerves tighten and her body start to pulse with the strangest feelings…

Jordan put the glass down with a small clatter which made her jump. Her eyes flew to his face and she felt heat sweep through her as she saw the expression in his eyes, the light which seemed to burn in their slumberous depths…

'Katherine…are you listening?'

'Yes, yes…I'm sorry.' She took a swift breath as her father claimed her attention again. She turned back to face the wall, wondering what was wrong with her that she should be noticing things which would have passed by her before.

'What did you mean about *warning* you that Jordan would be there? There's nothing wrong, is there, Katherine? You and Jordan aren't having problems?'

'No, of course not!' Katherine somehow managed a shaky laugh as she realised how the chance remark had

worried her father. 'I can't imagine where you got such
an idea!'

'Are you sure? I've had a feeling lately that maybe
things aren't quite right with you two.' Adam hesitated.
'I've always worried that what happened with your
mother and I might have affected you in some way, darling, if you want to know the truth.'

Katherine's heart turned over when she heard what
her father said. She closed her eyes in an agony of pain
as she realised how close to the truth it was. 'Of...of
course not, Daddy. Don't be silly.'

'So you and Jordan are happy, then?'

'Yes...yes, very happy.' She hurriedly changed the
subject. Lying to her father had never been easy, and it
seemed harder than ever when she knew deep down that
things had never been worse between her and Jordan.
'Anyhow, to get back to why you rang, the wedding
went perfectly, Daddy. It was such a glorious day and
Diane looked lovely.'

She tried to focus on the conversation, only to swing
round in alarm as she heard Jordan come up behind her.
He smiled as he reached past her to take cups out of the
cupboard. He was so close that she could feel the
warmth of his body all down the length of hers, smell
the faintly musky scent of his skin...

Her heart raced as she turned back to face the wall,
her hand clenching on the telephone cord. 'It's just a
pity that you couldn't be there. But there were lots of
photographs taken so you'll be able to see them, of
course.'

She knew that she was gabbling, but it seemed pref-
erable to fill the silence rather than allow her imagination
any more leeway. 'Mind you, Peter wasn't at his best.
He was too worried for that.'

'Worried? What about? He isn't in some sort of trouble, is he?'

Too late she realised what she had said, but it was impossible to take the words back. She closed her eyes in panic as she wondered what to reply. The last thing she wanted was for her father to find out the truth in his state of health!

A hand lifted the phone from her trembling fingers, and Katherine's eyes flew open. Jordan pressed a finger to his lips then held the receiver to his ear. 'Adam, how are you?'

Katherine had no idea what her father replied because all she could hear was the drumming of her heart deafening her to everything else. By necessity, Jordan was standing so close that their bodies were touching, the coiled length of the telephone wire not allowing much movement. He suddenly leant towards the wall, using his free hand to steady himself, effectively trapping Katherine in the narrow gap.

Her gaze was drawn instantly to the open front of his robe, to the gleaming bronze of his skin beneath that pelt of springy dark hair...

Her hands clenched, but the tingling in her palms didn't lessen in any way. It was as though she could feel the soft rasp of hair against her fingers, as she had felt it last night.

Katherine took a shaky breath and looked sharply downwards, but knew that was a mistake almost immediately. Jordan couldn't have secured the belt of the robe tightly enough, because now the front edges barely met. Through the gap she could see one long, strong thigh...

'Katherine?' Jordan's voice was husky, but the amusement in it was tempered by something far more dangerous. Her head shot up and she stared at him a little wildly before she realised that he was offering her the receiver.

She took it from him with a hand that shook, trying to blot out everything apart from her father's voice, but she was instantly aware the moment Jordan moved away.

'I shall really look forward to the weekend now, knowing that you'll be coming to stay. What a lovely idea, darling!'

Adam Carstairs sounded buoyant now; his previous concern about Peter had completely disappeared. Katherine didn't know what Jordan had said, but it had done the trick. However, she had no idea what her father meant about the weekend.

'I'm sorry, Daddy. I'm not following you. What did you mean about our staying the weekend?'

Adam laughed in obvious amusement. 'Mmm, your head does seem to be in the clouds this morning! And I imagine I can guess why that is. Still, it does prove how silly I've been to worry. I'm sure the only thing wrong is that you and Jordan spend far too much time apart. It will do you both good to have this week together, and now there's the weekend to look forward to as well.

'Do you realise that you two have never been down to stay with me together in the whole of the time you've been married? It's about time we changed all that.'

Katherine felt a wave of panic hit her as she glanced over her shoulder, but Jordan had his back to her as he poured coffee. Surely he hadn't told her father that they would both go to stay with him? It was out of the question!

'I…I'm sorry, Daddy, but there is no way we can come and stay.'

'Why on earth not?'

Because my marriage is a sham! Katherine wanted to reply. Because I cannot, will not, sleep in the same bed as my husband...

But she had slept in the same bed as him last night, hadn't she?

She took a jerky breath and blanked out that thought; she was not proof against it at that moment, when her nerves were so raw. 'Because...because Jordan might not be well enough to travel,' she improvised hurriedly. 'He obviously never thought to mention the fact that he hasn't been well, and I doubt he will be up to making the journey by then. Frankly, I don't know what he's doing getting up this morning!'

She shot an angry look over her shoulder and felt her temper surge as Jordan raised his cup in a mocking salute which seemed to disprove her claims. Apart from a faint weariness around the eyes he looked remarkably fit, considering how ill he had been just a few hours previously!

'Oh, I see. Well, of course you must wait and see how he is.' Adam tried to hide his disappointment. 'Don't even think about coming down unless Jordan is one hundred per cent fit. Promise me, darling?'

'Yes...yes, of course, Daddy.' Katherine sighed as she said goodbye and hung up. She hated to let her father down like that, even though it hadn't been she who had raised his hopes in the first place!

'Everything all right now, Katherine? I think I managed to convince Adam there was nothing to worry about.'

'No, it isn't all right!' She swung round, the light of battle flaring in her grey eyes. 'What on earth were you thinking of, making such arrangements, Jordan? Have you no idea of the difficulties involved in us spending a weekend together at my father's house?'

'Meaning, I imagine, all the questions which would be asked if we demanded separate rooms?' Jordan laughed softly but his gaze was intent. 'There is an easy answer to that, though, isn't there?'

'*Meaning* that we share the same room? I don't think so!'

'We shared one last night, Katherine. It wasn't that difficult.' He picked up his cup and swirled the coffee round. 'In fact, I would go so far as to say it was an arrangement which I would be quite happy to repeat.'

'Well, I wouldn't!' Katherine wrapped her arms around herself as a shiver danced down her spine, yet, oddly, she didn't feel cold—far from it. She could feel ripples of heat running under her skin, as though her blood had warmed by several degrees.

What had she seen on Jordan's face just now? Suddenly she didn't want to know, didn't want to admit even to the possibility that he had looked at her with desire in his eyes!

'Why not? Quite frankly I can't see what the problem is. When I woke up this morning you looked quite comfortable snuggled up beside me in bed, Katherine. I didn't get the impression that you were too bothered about being there.' He gave a softly reminiscent laugh, as though the memory pleased him. 'But then we *are* married, so it's hardly a sin to share the same bed, is it?'

Katherine's heart turned over. It made her feel incredibly vulnerable to imagine Jordan watching her while she slept, as she had watched him. 'Last night was...was different.'

'In what way?' He sounded puzzled, as though he

really wasn't sure what she meant, but she wasn't fool enough to believe that! Jordan knew that she would never have got into that bed if there hadn't been a genuine reason for doing so.

She drew herself up, her slender body quivering with outrage and a host of other emotions she refused to examine too closely right then. 'You know perfectly well what I mean. Now, if you'll excuse me, I have things to do other than stand here playing games with you.'

She started past him, only to come to an abrupt halt as he caught hold of her hand. His fingers were warm and dry as they closed around hers, his skin slightly abrasive. She shot an angry look downwards, about to demand that he let her go, but he had already started speaking in a voice which was so soft and deep that it kept her silent.

'Last night I was ill. I remember very clearly how cold I felt when the fever passed, how impossible it was for me to get warm. And then you got into bed with me, Katherine, and took me in your arms and held me close. I imagine it didn't take all that long to warm me up, did it? So why didn't you leave then? Why did you stay with me all night?'

'I…' Katherine stared blindly down at his hand while the question drummed inside her head. Why hadn't she got up out of bed the very moment she knew that he'd settled? Because…because she had fallen asleep, feeling safe and secure with Jordan lying beside her.

The answer shocked her, and she could feel the blood pounding at her temples, the wave of dizziness which washed over her. How could she have felt safe when the thought of sharing a bed with Jordan was the thing which had scared her most this past year?

She struggled to find an explanation which both of

them would believe. 'Last night you were ill, Jordan, and…and…'

'And incapable of taking advantage of you?' He finished drily before he laughed huskily. 'I see. So that's it? You wouldn't trust me not to do so at any other time—not if I was in full health, right?'

Katherine snatched her hand away, her face flaming at his teasing. 'No! If you want the truth, then I wouldn't trust you in *any* other circumstances! Now, if you have quite finished having your fun…'

She stormed towards the door, then slowed down when Jordan said quietly, 'Maybe it isn't me you don't trust, though, Katherine.'

'I don't know what you mean.' She swung round, her heart thundering as she saw the way he was watching her.

'Of course you do. After all, what happened on our wedding night wasn't just down to me, was it? You were just as eager as I was until you realised what you were doing and where it would lead to.' He paused deliberately, his gaze hard and unyielding as he studied her. 'Maybe you're afraid that next time you won't be able to call a halt.'

'No! You're wrong, Jordan. Wrong!' Her voice was hoarse with pain, the fear she felt sweeping through her in huge, icy waves. 'I feel nothing for you—understand? Nothing at all!'

She searched his face, desperate to see some sign that she had convinced him, but he stared straight back at her, his eyes glittering with a certainty that showed her he didn't believe a word of what she'd said.

Katherine turned and blindly left the room, closing the door behind her as though by doing so she could shut what Jordan had said out of her mind—but it was impossible to do that when it was true.

She could never again trust herself not to be seduced by that passion they had shared, yet if she gave into it again it could end up destroying her!

It was almost seven when Katherine let herself into the flat. She had spent the day walking aimlessly around the shops, unable to face the thought of going back and seeing Jordan again after what had happened that morning. She had been half tempted to book into a hotel before it struck her that she *had* to see him again.

There was still the problem of what he was going to do about Peter to be resolved, although the thought of making Jordan come round to her way of thinking was almost more than she felt able to face right then!

She sighed as she slipped off her jacket and went to her room to hang it up. She glanced in the mirror, then picked up a brush and ran it through her hair. Her face looked pale and wan in the glass, uncertainty darkening her eyes to a stormy grey which reflected her inner turmoil.

Could she convince Jordan to see sense? Or would he insist on keeping to the terms he had outlined last night before he agreed to help Peter? It was the uncertainty which was worse, the not knowing what he was going to do. Jordan had been acting so strangely lately that it was hard to know what he would do about anything!

Katherine glanced along the hall as she left her room, suddenly realising how quiet it was. The spare-room door was closed, making her wonder fleetingly if she should go and check that Jordan was all right. But she strode determinedly into the sitting-room. She would check how he was later. Right now she needed a bit more breathing space, despite the hours she'd already had!

Katherine was just pouring herself a glass of sherry when the doorbell rang. She set the decanter down, wondering who it could be. She rarely had visitors nowadays because in the past year she had let any friendships lapse. It had seemed easier than answering all sorts of curious questions. Her friends might have found something decidedly odd about the amount of time Jordan spent away from his new bride, not to mention how happy that said bride was with the arrangement.

Katherine hurried to the door and gasped in surprise as she opened it. 'Charles! Good heavens, what are you doing here?'

'I thought I'd just call round, seeing as I was passing. I'm not disturbing you, I hope, Katherine?'

There was a fleeting uncertainty in his brown eyes but Katherine hastened to reassure him. 'Of course not! It's always lovely to see you, Charles. Come in, please.'

She held the door open with a genuinely warm smile. Charles Langtree was the one friend she was always happy to see. Katherine knew that it was partly because he never asked any awkward questions and partly because he always treated her with an old-fashioned courtesy she appreciated. He was a little older than Jordan— somewhere in his mid-forties, Katherine guessed— although he had the sort of boyish good looks which made him appear a lot younger.

Jordan had introduced them when Katherine had gone to his office one day. She had taken an immediate liking to Jordan's operations manager, helped by the fact that she and Charles shared several friends as well as a lot of the same interests.

Over the past year Charles had been to the flat several

times for a drink, before they had gone out to the ballet
or the opera, and had even had supper with her on the
odd occasion. They had been pleasant little interludes
which Katherine had enjoyed, although she couldn't recall him ever calling round to see her without telephoning first.

She led him into the sitting-room and closed the door
so that they wouldn't disturb Jordan if he was asleep.
'Do sit down, Charles. Can I get you anything? I was
just about to have a glass of sherry—or perhaps you'd
prefer something stronger?'

He shook his head. 'No, I'd better not. I already had
a couple of large whiskies before I came here.' He grimaced as he ran his hand through his slightly greying
fair hair. 'Mind you, with the day I've just had, I don't
think a whole damned bottle would have helped!'

'Good heavens, that sounds rather ominous.'
Katherine frowned as she sat down on the sofa. 'Is there
something wrong?'

'Oh, just a few problems which have taken a bit of
sorting out.' Charles sighed. 'Of course, if I could have
got hold of Jordan then I'm sure he could have solved
them in a fraction of the time it took me! I put umpteen
calls through to his hotel in Tokyo, but all I kept getting
was some receptionist telling me he wasn't there. He did
mention something about being invited to Tashimoko's
home, so I expect that's where he's gone.

'Still, I didn't come here to bore you with my problems, Katherine. I came to throw myself on your good
nature and see if you would come out to dinner with me.
I could do with cheering up, believe me!'

'It's a pity you didn't call sooner, Charles, then you
wouldn't be in such desperate need of cheering!'

Katherine laughed as she saw his confusion. 'Jordan is here. Didn't you know? He arrived back on...'

She stopped as she heard the door opening, the smile freezing on her lips as she looked round and caught the full force of Jordan's icy glare. He came into the room and quietly closed the door behind him, and Katherine wondered rather wildly how such a simple act could seem so very menacing!

CHAPTER SIX

'So, CHARLES, this is the way you spend your evenings, is it?'

Jordan's tone was light enough, but Katherine knew that she wasn't the only one to hear the cutting edge to it. She looked at Charles and saw the colour wash up his face as he hurriedly got to his feet.

'I had no idea you were here, Jordan.' He cleared his throat hastily, his colour deepening. 'What I meant was that I didn't know you were back in England.'

'No?' Jordan's black brows rose. He was a good head taller than the other man, and far more powerfully built, so he seemed to dwarf Charles as he moved into the middle of the room and stared at him with a coldness Katherine couldn't understand.

'Then obviously you didn't come here to see me, did you, Charles? In that case I can only assume that you came to see Katherine.' He gave a throaty laugh which held little trace of amusement. 'I hope I haven't spoiled your plans by being here?'

His eyes swept from Charles to Katherine, and she felt her own face heat as she saw the icy contempt etched in them. She looked away and ran a nervous hand down her pleated navy skirt, hearing a matching nervousness in Charles's voice as he replied just a shade too heartily.

'Of course not! Good heavens, I don't know where you got that idea from. I'm glad you're back, to tell you the truth, Jordan. I wish I'd known you were here sooner.'

'I'm sure you do. Forewarned is forearmed, or so they say, Charles.' There was cynical amusement in Jordan's deep voice as he sat down on the sofa beside Katherine. He slid his arm along its back, his fingers brushing the nape of her neck, although whether by accident or design she had no idea.

He had obviously just showered before dressing in slim-fitting black jeans and a pale blue shirt because she could smell the scent of the soap he always used. Unbidden, her mind shot back to the previous day, to those moments in the bathroom as she had helped him to his feet...

'What? Oh, yes, yes, so they do.'

Charles gave an uneasy laugh and Katherine blanked out her thoughts as she realised that poor Charles was starting to look decidedly uncomfortable at being the only one still standing. She shot a quelling look at Jordan, annoyed that he should be acting so rudely, but he stared even more coldly back at her.

She looked away abruptly and forced a smile, but she couldn't shake off the feeling that Jordan was furiously angry about something. 'Do sit down, Charles. Are you sure you wouldn't like a drink? Or coffee, perhaps? It won't take me a moment to make some, really.'

'Er, no...no, I'd better not. Thank you anyway, Katherine.' He shot back his cuff and made a great show of checking his watch. 'Good Lord, is it that time already? I hadn't realised. I think I'd better be on my way.' He looked at Jordan and shifted uncomfortably. 'There were one or two problems which cropped up this morning. I did try to get in touch with you, but obviously I couldn't. I've done what I thought was best so hopefully everything is settled.'

'I hope so too. After all, that's what I pay you for,

Charles—to handle any problems which crop up in my absence. There would be little point in keeping you on if you weren't up to the job.' Jordan let the words hang heavily for a moment before he continued smoothly, 'I shall expect a full report on everything that has happened while I've been away to be on my desk first thing in the morning.'

Charles opened his mouth, then obviously thought better of saying what he had been going to say. However, there was a tightness to his mouth which told Katherine that he wasn't pleased, and who could blame him? The way Jordan had spoken to him was outrageous.

She got to her feet and followed Charles from the room, wondering what on earth was the matter with Jordan that he should act like that. Charles turned to her as they reached the front door with an expression of concern on his face.

'I do hope that my coming here hasn't made things...well, awkward, Katherine.' He shot a glance towards the sitting-room and she saw him grimace. 'Jordan can be rather difficult at times.'

'Of course not!' Katherine summoned up a small laugh, but it was rather too thin to be convincing. 'Difficult' didn't even begin to describe Jordan in her view! 'And please don't be offended by the way Jordan behaved, Charles. He isn't himself right now. I'm sure he didn't mean to be rude.'

She saw Charles's disbelief and laid her hand on his arm, wanting to convince him. 'Jordan isn't well. In fact, I don't think he should even be out of bed. According to the doctor I had to call yesterday, he's suffering from malaria. Heaven knows, that must be enough to make anyone grumpy!'

She brushed Charles's cheek with an affectionate kiss, pleased to see that he looked somewhat happier as he turned to wave before stepping into the lift. Katherine sighed as she closed the door. Maybe Jordan wasn't well, but did that explain the way he had acted?

She turned to go back to the sitting-room, then stopped as she saw Jordan standing in the doorway. Her hand flew to her chest to quiet the sudden leap her heart gave, and she saw him smile narrowly.

'I hope you weren't too disappointed that Charles decided not to stay, Katherine. You should have mentioned that he was going to call and I would have had the drinks ready.'

'I had no idea that he was coming,' she said flatly.

She felt a shiver run down her spine as she felt his eyes bore into her.

'No? So Charles is in the habit of just dropping round whenever he pleases? How cosy. But then Charles is a *friend*, isn't he, Katherine? Why shouldn't he pop round for a drink, maybe even a meal?' Jordan folded his arms and leant against the wall. He smiled, but Katherine could see the anger in his eyes, feel the tension which seemed to fill the small hallway. 'Has Charles been here for dinner, Katherine?'

Katherine rubbed her suddenly damp palms down the seams of her skirt. 'A couple of times before we went out to the opera. Why? Is there any reason why he shouldn't have been?'

She moved along the hall and Jordan stepped aside so that she could pass him, but he made no attempt to follow her into the sitting-room. Katherine picked up her glass, then set it down again without drinking any of the sherry as she swung round to face him. 'What is this all about, Jordan? You were unforgivably rude to Charles just now!'

'Rude? I don't recall saying anything I shouldn't have. Charles is an employee, Katherine. I know exactly where he comes in the order of things. It's just a pity that it appears you don't.'

His voice grated. Katherine felt it rub rawly against nerves which were already far too exposed. 'And what is that supposed to mean? It was obvious to both of us that something was bothering you even before you started your interrogation about the number of times Charles has been to the flat!' She gave a sharp little laugh, the colour settling in an angry line along her cheekbones. 'I tried explaining away your rudeness by telling Charles how ill you've been, but I doubt that is the real explanation for your behaviour!'

Jordan's eyes glittered with fury as he took a few long strides which brought him into the room. 'I don't need you or anyone else apologising for me, Katherine! Understand?'

His tone flicked at her nerves again, sending a matching anger racing through her. Katherine could feel it spreading through her whole body, and any thoughts she might have had about the wisdom of goading him like this fled abruptly.

'No? Then if you don't need anyone making apologies for you may I suggest you try acting a little more civilised rather than like the barbarian you obviously are?'

She went to walk past him, refusing to stay in the room and trade words with a man who appeared not to understand the rudiments of civilised behaviour. However, with a speed which made her gasp, Jordan caught her by the shoulders and spun her round to face him.

'More like Charles, do you mean? Does the way he behaves conform more to your ideas, Katherine?' His laughter was harsh and cruel, his blue eyes blazing as he bent to stare into her face. 'Is that what you prefer, my sweet? A man who is willing to let you walk all over him? What a pity that the man you married isn't like that! But then there *are* some things about me you like— although on second thoughts perhaps "like" isn't the right word.'

His fingers were hard as he forced her head up, his eyes holding a light which made her heart still. '"Respond" is a much better word. It conjures up a far different picture, don't you agree? And in certain respects, Katherine, you *respond* to me more than you could ever respond to Charles or any other of his ilk!'

'No! How dare you? Jordan, stop…!'

She got no further. The angry, fearful words were stopped on her lips by the harsh pressure of Jordan's mouth as he kissed her.

Katherine kept her eyes open, staring into his as she willed him to stop what he was doing, but it made no difference. His eyes blazed back into hers, the fire she could see burning in them fed by his anger and something else—something which made her legs go so weak that she could barely stand, something which made her heart start to beat so heavily that she could feel herself shaking with it. She didn't want to see that desire in Jordan's eyes; she couldn't bear it!

Katherine closed her eyes on a whimper of fear and felt Jordan draw her closer, so that her body was locked against his. She could feel her breasts pressing against the hard wall of his chest now, the tiny, panting breaths she was taking making them rise and fall so that her nipples brushed up and down against it. She felt them tighten in immediate, helpless response, and, in a frenzy of fear and outrage, beat her fists against his shoulders to make him free her.

Jordan raised his head at last, his arms still imprisoning her against him, his lips parting in a smile that held undisguised triumph. 'See what I mean, sweet Kate? You respond to me. You actually *feel* something!'

'I hate you, Jordan! Do you hear me? I hate you!' Katherine's voice was hoarse. She glared into his eyes, wanting there to be no doubt in his mind as to how she felt about him!

He laughed deeply, and laughed again as he saw the shock which crossed her face as she heard him. 'Hate me all you like, Katherine! Loathe me, detest me, feel for me everything you have never allowed yourself to feel before. I don't give a damn how much you hate me, if you want the truth, because at least you're feeling something! And that has to be a hell of a lot better than feeling nothing at all!'

'No...' She didn't know what to say, didn't know what to think; she didn't know what she was feeling any more, even.

Katherine stared into his fiery blue eyes, and she felt her heart jerk to a stop as he reached up and gently brushed her mouth with his knuckles in the lightest of caresses which she could feel echoing in every pulse-point. 'Jordan...no...please...'

'Shh, Katherine, don't say anything. It just confuses things. Just let yourself feel for once, and then maybe you'll realise what I want you to understand most of all.'

His voice was little more than a murmur, so the words seemed dream-like. Had he said them? Had she heard them? Or had her mind simply conjured them up out of the charged air? Katherine couldn't decide—didn't have time to before she saw Jordan bend towards her.

His mouth was so gentle as it touched hers this time that moving away from its softness seemed like a sin. Katherine let her eyes drift shut, as though by doing so she could pretend it wasn't happening, but it was impossible to curtail her other senses so easily.

Jordan's lips were cool and firm against hers, yet she sensed the heat that burned beneath...

She tried to blank that thought out, but suddenly the scent of his skin was overwhelming, the fresh tang of the soap he used, the musky fragrance of man...

She blocked her mind to the aromas. But now there was the rasping sound of his breathing to contend with, and the way it mingled with hers to make a very special kind of music...

She was awash with sensations now, and the realisation of how vulnerable she was was just too much. Katherine felt tears gather behind her closed lids and seep down her cheeks. They ran over their joined mouths and she felt Jordan's lips part, then the warm sweep of his tongue against her mouth as he licked them away.

The final wave hit her so forcefully that she gasped— and felt the gentle intrusion of his tongue as it slipped between her parted lips, salty with the taste of her tears. Katherine moaned sharply, overwhelmed by the desire which flared inside her then, by the force of the passion she felt as she kissed him back. She was burning with it, drowning in it, breathing it, tasting it; it was a passion she had known only once before, a passion she didn't dare feel again!

He didn't try to stop her as she pushed him away. He simply stood and looked at her, and the knowledge of what he was seeing made her feel raw. She stumbled to her room and lay down on the bed, trying not to listen to the voice which whispered inside her head, but it was impossible to shut it out.

She wanted Jordan to make love to her... It would be so easy to let it happen... And then the nightmare would begin...

'Katherine...are you there?'

Katherine froze as she heard Jordan calling her. She shot a glance to the mirror, desperate to check that the turmoil she had been going through for the past hour didn't show. The night was warm and she had changed into a sleeveless dress of black silk, its elegant lines just hinting at the soft curves beneath.

On the outside, at least, she looked in control, but she knew it was just a thin veneer which wouldn't withstand too much pressure...

'Katherine!'

She took a deep breath as she heard the growing impatience in his voice, and went to open the bedroom door. 'Yes?'

His blue eyes travelled the length of her slender body in the plain black dress before he turned away abruptly. 'I've made us a meal. I'll start serving it if you're ready.'

Katherine let out her pent-up breath as she watched him disappear into the kitchen. 'Ready' didn't describe her state of mind right then! She glanced back towards the sanctuary of her room, then slowly followed him. She would have to face him some time, and it was probably better that she got it over with, but that didn't make it any easier.

She felt herself start to tremble as fear rose inside her again. Would Jordan refer to what had happened before? Would he taunt her with the way she had responded?

Could…could she find some way to explain it away when they both knew the truth?

'Come in, Katherine. I won't bite.' Jordan smiled thinly as he saw her hesitating in the doorway. 'I'm not a complete ogre, despite what you believe. If you're worried about fending off a repeat performance then don't be. I have no intention of pressing my unwanted attentions upon you again tonight!'

Katherine's face flamed as she felt the sting in the words. Jordan's attentions hadn't been unwanted in the end. That was the trouble! She looked away from his mocking eyes and sat down at the table, wondering how she was going to get through the rest of the evening.

'I hope you like omelettes. I'm afraid my culinary repertoire doesn't stretch to anything fancy.'

Jordan put a plate in front of her and she jumped violently. She kept her eyes locked on the table in case he saw how nervous she was, but she should have realised that he wouldn't allow her even that much leeway.

'Stop it!' He reached out and tilted her chin so that he could look into her eyes, and she felt a shiver ripple through her as she saw the expression in his. To see such bitterness in his gaze startled her, because she didn't understand what was causing it.

'I promise you here and now, Katherine, that I shall never again do what I did before. I regret it, and I apologise if I scared you in any way. You don't have to sit there looking as though you're expecting me to leap on you!'

His deep voice grated, and Katherine was shocked to hear the self-disgust which echoed in it. She watched in silence as he took his place, trying to understand what had caused it. Did Jordan really regret what had happened before? It didn't make sense. She'd thought that he'd wanted to teach her a lesson and would be feeling pleased at having achieved that objective so effectively!

Her hand shook as she picked up her glass and took a sip of the chilled white wine, but the wine didn't help. She set it down again, the questions humming inside her head and demanding answers even though she knew it was foolish to ask them.

'Why did you do it, Jordan?'

Her voice was soft, yet she saw his hands clench before he laid down his knife and fork. 'Why do you think?'

She shrugged, looking down at her plate as though the sight of the omelette fascinated her. 'Because you wanted to teach me a lesson, prove a point...? I'm not sure which.'

He gave a soft laugh which made her eyes fly to his face in surprise as she heard the wry note in it. 'Mmm, I wish I could claim it was either or both of those, but it would be a lie, Katherine. I behaved the way I did for the most basest of reasons, if you want the truth. I was jealous.'

'Jealous?' Katherine heard the shock in her voice, a reflection of how she felt right then. She stared at him with eyes full of bewilderment. 'Jealous of what?' She gasped. 'Of Charles?'

Jordan stared darkly down at his wineglass. 'Yes, of Charles.' He looked up suddenly and his eyes blazed. 'You are my wife. How do you expect me to feel when I keep hearing about the amount of time you and Charles are spending together?'

It was a question she couldn't answer for any number of reasons. Katherine stared at him, dumbfounded both by the accusation and what lay behind it.

His wife! She couldn't recall Jordan ever making that

claim before, not so…so possessively! It stunned her to realise that was how he felt. She had always imagined that he viewed their relationship with the same detachment she tried to employ—but the tone of his voice and the words he had used disputed that!

'Charles is…well, he's just a friend,' she managed at last, wondering why she felt the need to make him understand that—wondering also why she felt a frisson of pleasure run under her skin at the thought that Jordan cared enough to lay claim to her the way he had. 'I explained that before, and it's true. I enjoy his company and we get on well together, but there has never been anything more than that to it.'

'And are you sure that's how Charles feels? That he views your relationship simply as a cosy little friendship?' Jordan drank some wine, then gave a harsh laugh which made her flinch. 'I don't think so, Katherine. I think Charles is getting some very different ideas in his head!'

'No! That's ridiculous. Charles knows that I am married to you. That fact alone is enough to ensure he understands the situation.' Katherine sat up straighter, hating the way that Jordan was putting her on the defensive. 'Charles has never been anything other than polite and courteous. He has never made any attempt to…to…'

'Kiss you? Make love to you? Break through that wall of ice which is such a challenge to any red-blooded male? Maybe he hasn't yet, but he will—take it from me, Katherine. And I want it to stop now, before it gets out of hand and I'm forced to take steps to end it.'

'Steps? What sort of steps?' Her voice was tight, the words almost too difficult to utter, her disbelief at what she was hearing total. 'What are you saying, Jordan?'

'That Charles could find it extremely difficult to get

another job as well paid as the one he has working for me. Am I making myself clear enough now?'

'Perfectly! I just can't believe that I am hearing this, though! You're really threatening to sack Charles just because he's been such a loyal friend to me?' Katherine pushed back her chair, any appetite she'd had swept away by Jordan's arrogance. 'How dare you try to tell me whom I can and can't see? How dare you try to dictate my life like this? Just who do you think you are?'

'Your husband, that's who!' He rose to his feet, his eyes blazing at her across the table. 'And it's about time you tried remembering that!'

Katherine stared at him in shock, seeing the way his mouth was drawn into a tight line of fury, how a nerve was beating wildly along his jaw. Jordan looked within a hair's breadth of losing control, and she wasn't sure she could handle him if he did.

Suddenly he swayed, and the colour drained from his face. Katherine could see the struggle he was having to stay on his feet as he gripped hold of the table. Her anger disappeared at once as she rushed round to help him.

'Sit down. I'll get you some water.' She helped him into a chair then hurried to the sink, filled a glass with water and took it back to him. 'Here, drink this.'

He took the glass, and she was alarmed to see how his hand shook. It was obvious that he had pushed himself too hard today, so maybe that explained his unreasonable attitude. She was prepared to accept that. In fact, she *preferred* to accept that explanation rather than look for another.

'You shouldn't be out of bed, by the look of you. You know you aren't better yet.'

'I hate being ill.' His expression was wry as he looked at her, hinting at how he felt about displaying such weakness. Jordan was a man who made few allowances for anyone, and even less for himself. He drove himself far too hard, Katherine thought suddenly, pushed himself beyond any sensible limits. It made her wonder what he was trying to prove.

'I'm a rotten patient, Katherine, so be warned.' There was the same wryness in his voice as she had seen on his face, and it helped ease the tension.

'You don't have to tell me that!' She managed a shaky smile. 'I can see for myself that you must be a nurse's nightmare, but you have to be sensible, Jordan. Malaria is a little more severe than the common cold!'

He shrugged, looking faintly arrogant as his colour returned. 'It's only as bad as you allow it to be. I'll be right as rain by tomorrow. It usually only takes a couple of days before the worst has passed.'

'Of course, you've had it before, haven't you? So how did you get it in the first place?' she asked curiously.

'Out in Africa about fifteen years ago.' He drained the glass, then set it down with a grimace. 'Considering the conditions we were working under, it's surprising that more of us didn't come down with it. As it was, there were at least a dozen of us sick, and we had a pretty rough time. It's been a few years since I had a bout of it, though, which is why it didn't register at first what was wrong.'

'I see.' Katherine picked up the glass and went to refill it. One part of her couldn't quite believe that they were having this conversation, after what had just happened, while the rest of her was glad. She hated confrontation of any kind, which was why she tried so hard to remain detached, yet it was incredibly difficult to behave like that around Jordan. He had a way of igniting her temper...

But then he had a way of igniting all sorts of feelings inside her, didn't he?

Katherine felt the colour sweep up her cheeks as she set the glass down on the table. She took a steadying breath to calm herself down, and rushed into speech. 'So what were you doing in Africa? It doesn't sound as though you were there for a holiday.'

He gave a low laugh which held a note that told her he understood she was trying to change the subject. 'I wasn't! I was out there working on a new road which was being constructed.'

'One of your firm's projects?'

'No, this was before I set my company up. I was working for someone else.' He shrugged. 'There was always a lot of work like that available because nobody wanted to go out to places where conditions were less than basic. I was there overseeing some of the local workforce.'

'It doesn't sound very pleasant, so why did you do it?'

'Why do you imagine?' Jordan looked at her with a grimace. 'Money, of course. The pay was always good on those projects because quite apart from the living conditions there was always the chance that you'd get caught up in some sort of local conflict between one faction and another. People weren't exactly queuing up to take the jobs when they were advertised.'

'I can understand that! But why did you need money so desperately that you were prepared to take such a risk? It must have been incredibly dangerous work.' Katherine couldn't hide her surprise, and she saw him smile grimly.

'It was, at times, but I needed the money I earned out

there to pay my way through college. Without it I wouldn't be where I am today. It's as simple as that.'

'But surely your family could have helped rather than you running the risk of getting hurt? Or were your parents dead by then?'

Katherine frowned, trying to think back over what she knew about him. It was so little, that was the trouble. Her knowledge was confined to what she had read in the papers, because she and Jordan had never really discussed his past life. It had never seemed important before. She knew enough about him to get by and to avoid any awkward questions. Yet suddenly she realised that she wanted to learn more about him. Why? What had changed? She wasn't sure but she knew deep down that something had.

'I know from what I've read that your parents are dead, although I have no idea how long ago they died,' she said hesitantly.

'Neither have I.' He must have heard the gasp she gave because he smiled cynically. 'In fact, I don't really know if they *are* dead. It seemed easier to put that story around when the press started asking questions about me rather than tell them the truth.'

'The truth?' Katherine echoed numbly.

'That I have no idea what happened to them.' He stared down at the glass, and Katherine had the feeling that he was trying to decide what to tell her.

He had obviously made up his mind. He looked up and his gaze was hard, yet she sensed that it was merely a mask for what he was really feeling.

'I don't know who my father was, Katherine, because he disappeared from the scene before I was born. As for my mother...' He shrugged. 'I remember her vaguely. I must have been about six when I saw her last. She had me taken into care when she remarried. Evidently her new husband didn't want me around, so that was that. I don't know where she is or even if she is dead or alive, because I have never bothered trying to find out. She went out of my life too long ago for it to make any difference now.'

'But that's dreadful! How could she do that? How could she abandon you when you were so young?' Katherine was horrified, yet, in a way, what had happened to Jordan was simply an echo of what had happened to her.

Katherine had been fifteen when her mother had left home. She had understood only too well what was going on, and it had been a relief when Caroline Carstairs had left. But of course her father had been there, rock-solid in his devotion to her and Peter. Jordan had had no one to turn to, though, no one to comfort him.

Without thinking, Katherine reached across the table and laid her hand on his. 'It must have been awful for you, Jordan,' she said softly.

'It wasn't easy.' Jordan turned his hand over to capture hers as his eyes rose to her face, and something inside her wept at the bleakness she saw there, an echo of the lost, abandoned child he had been.

'I was placed with dozens of foster-families over the years, but each time they sent me back to the home. It wasn't their fault. I didn't make it easy for them to love me, or even just to want me, Katherine. I was in and out of trouble as I grew up, and it might have ended up a hell of a lot worse if I hadn't gone into the Army when I was eighteen. That taught me discipline and a sense of self-worth I'd never had before. It also showed me what I wanted to do with my life.'

'Engineering?' she suggested, quietly, and saw him smile.

'Yes. I realised that what I wanted more than anything was to build things—beautiful, useful things like bridges and roads which would last and make life easier for people. The only problem was that I needed the right qualifications, and getting them cost money.'

'Surely you would have been able to get a grant or something?'

'Oh, yes, I was entitled to that. But it was all the extras I needed the cash for—the books, the trips abroad to study major engineering projects, a whole host of things. I wanted to be the best, Katherine. I wouldn't accept anything less!'

He smoothed his thumb over her knuckles, his touch so light that it seemed more like a whisper of sensation, yet Katherine felt it in every cell.

She drew her hand away, suddenly aware of what she was doing, and he didn't try to stop her. There was a deep weariness in his eyes as they rested on her, almost as though he had expected her to react like that.

'My background is a world removed from yours, Katherine. I'm not proud of some of the things I've done, but I can't change them. Given the same set of circumstances, I would do exactly the same again.

'I've never had time to learn about the arts and music, all the things you take so much for granted. I've had to fight for everything I have, and I imagine it has left its mark on me. I am who I am, Katherine, and maybe you were right to call me a barbarian before. All I can say is that I did what I had to, and…well, the rest is history, so they say.'

He got up and carried his plate over to the wastebin to scrape the cold food into it.

Katherine watched him in silence although her mind was racing. Jordan might have brushed off the rest of the story but she could fill in the gaps well enough. It must have taken a lot of determination to get where he was today. He'd had no connections to help him, none of that network of friends and acquaintances in the right places. The route to the top had been a steep uphill climb, but Jordan had made it all by himself.

He turned to look at her suddenly, and his gaze was intent despite the seeming lightness of his tone. 'So, Katherine, it isn't a particularly pleasant story, is it? I'm sure it hasn't done much to enhance your view of me.'

She picked up her own plate and got up. He stepped aside to let her pass, watching her from under lowered black brows. Katherine's hand shook so that the cutlery clattered against the china as she set the plate down on the counter.

'No, it isn't a pleasant story.' She saw his mouth thin, and smiled gently. 'But you should be proud of what you have achieved, Jordan. Few people could have done so well given the kind of obstacles you were up against.'

'Thank you.' His deep voice hummed, and Katherine got the impression that he wanted to say something more but couldn't bring himself to do so. She understood. Jordan was a proud man and he would never beg anyone to accept him for what he was, yet the fact that she had pleased him deeply.

For a moment they stared at one another in silence, and then she took a slow breath. Tonight she had learned so much about Jordan that she had been ignorant of before, and, like it or not, it did change the way she saw him. The Jordan James she'd thought she knew had become someone else—a man who aroused her sympathy, a man whom she admired, a man who was so much more than the person she had married simply to save her father!

Katherine felt the shock ripple coldly under her skin as she realised what a mistake it had been to let curiosity get the better of her. She could no longer view Jordan with indifference, and that was the biggest mistake she could have made!

'If…if you'll excuse me, I think I'll go to bed now. I'm rather tired.'

Her voice sounded hollow, the words mocking her by their very politeness. Such a cool little statement, which came nowhere near hiding all the turbulence she felt right then!

'Of course. In fact, that's what I'm going to do. I shall take your advice, Katherine, and go to bed as well.'

Jordan's tone was just as bland, yet Katherine could hear the awareness in it and it scared her. Jordan knew that what he had told her had changed things, so would he try to use it to his advantage in some way?

She hurried from the kitchen, but he was right behind her as she opened her bedroom door. She felt her heart jolt as she looked round and found him watching her with gentle amusement. Jordan knew how confused she felt; she was in no doubt of that!

'Goodnight, Katherine. Sleep well.' His voice dropped an octave. 'Although I doubt either of us will sleep as well as we did last night.'

Katherine hurried into her room, almost slamming the door behind her in her haste to shut Jordan out on the other side. She closed her eyes as a wave of fear enveloped her.

Nothing was going to be the same after today—not how she felt, how Jordan acted, the life they had led since they'd been married! Everything had changed and she didn't think she could handle it!

It was only when she was lying in bed a short time later that it struck her that they hadn't discussed what was going to happen about Peter. That was going to change things even more!

CHAPTER SEVEN

KATHERINE cursed as the zip up the back of her cream linen dress jammed. She tugged a little harder but it wouldn't budge either up or down now.

She glanced uncertainly towards the door. She'd heard Jordan moving around some while back, but had no idea what he was doing now. She had made coffee while he was safely out of the way and then had hurried back to her room to get dressed before he appeared. Now it seemed unlikely that she could achieve that objective without help!

She took a deep breath before opening the door, mentally shoring up her resolve. She had to put what Jordan had told her out of her mind and not allow it to influence her. She had come to that conclusion at some point during the sleepless night because it was the only course open to her. Although, suddenly, she couldn't help wondering *why* he had told her so much about himself when he had never made any attempt to do so before.

She hesitated as the uncertainties came rushing back. It wasn't only what he had told her about his past, though, was it? There was what he had said about being jealous of Charles, that possessive note in his voice as he had claimed her as his wife, the way...the way he had kissed her...

Katherine's head swam. She could have wept as she realised what a fool she was. How could she ignore what had happened when it had been a watershed? And now

95

that they had reached it everything was irrevocably changed...

'Good morning. I hope I didn't wake you. I tried to be quiet in case you were still asleep.'

Jordan's voice. Jordan suddenly there behind her! Katherine swung round, her face flaming when she saw his brows arch as though he found her reaction puzzling. Her hand tightened on the door handle as she suddenly wondered if he regretted what had happened yesterday as much as she did. Or had he known exactly what he was doing, and why?

'Looks like you need a hand there.' Jordan tossed the jacket he was holding onto the hall chair then calmly turned her round and gave the zip a gentle tug. 'Uh-huh, it seems to be well and truly jammed, doesn't it...? Ah, now I see what the trouble is.'

Katherine twisted round to look over her shoulder, then immediately wished she hadn't when she realised how close he was. He was bending towards her while he tried to work the zip free, his mouth just an inch away from hers...

She turned back at once, her body stiffening in an agony of embarrassment as she felt her heart start to pound. 'Leave it. It doesn't matter,' she ordered thinly.

He gave a husky laugh. She felt his warm breath on her backbone, where the gaping back of her dress had left it exposed. 'So you're going to walk round all day like that, are you, sweetheart? You might have to, because you won't be able to take the dress off unless I sort this out.'

His hands lifted to cup her rigid shoulders, and his voice was husky with amusement. 'Trust me, Katherine. I'm an engineer. This shouldn't prove too big a problem for me to handle!'

Katherine couldn't recall Jordan ever teasing her in such a way. It just proved how much things had changed that he did so now.

She stood rigidly as he started to work on the recalcitrant zip, then flinched as she felt his fingers brush up her spine. His hands stilled at once, his knuckles resting lightly against her backbone. 'Sorry. I didn't scratch you, did I?'

'No.' Her voice was faint because that was all she could manage right then. She could feel the tingling imprint of his fingers all down her back, almost as though he had been stroking her skin...

She closed her eyes as her mind started to spin with those pictures again—Jordan's tanned hands sliding over her skin, his fingers finding the indentation at the base of her spine just above the rounded cheeks of her bottom...

'The only way to solve this is to snap that thread off, I think. Just hold still, sweetheart.'

She had no idea what he meant until she felt his cheek brush against her, then the faint rasp of his teeth on her skin as he bit the thread off. Katherine closed her eyes, telling herself that it was panic she felt, nothing more. Yet she knew that that didn't explain the sensations which shimmered over her body right then; she knew deep down that there was more to it than that.

'That's got it.' Jordan drew the zip up and then moved away to pick up his jacket. He glanced round and Katherine could hear the laughter in his voice as he saw her still standing there. 'It's safe to move now, Katherine. I'm all finished.'

She turned to glare at him, knowing at once that he understood everything she'd been feeling—all the confusion and anger, all the...

She wouldn't allow herself to put a name to whatever else she felt!

She drew herself up, desperately trying to hide how she felt behind a mask of cool indifference, but it seemed harder than ever to slip it on. 'I take it that you're going to the office? Do you think that's wise?'

Jordan shrugged on his jacket, then ran a hand over his hair to push back a heavy lock which had fallen over his forehead. 'I feel fine, although I appreciate your concern. It's nice to know that you have my welfare at heart. We do seem to be making progress towards a better understanding, don't we? It should make things simpler in the long run.'

There was just something in the way he said that... Katherine frowned as she tried to understand what he meant, and suddenly it was only too clear. Her eyes flew to his and she went cold as she saw him smile.

'I wanted you to know all about my past, Katherine, because if you do decide to accept my terms for helping your brother then I don't want you coming to me in a year or so's time claiming that you want out of the agreement because you had no idea of the kind of man I am. If we do have a child then I shall never allow you to leave me for any reason! I won't let any child of mine go through what I did. Is that clear?'

Katherine stared back at him, hardly able to believe that anyone could be so...so calculating! 'Yes, it's clear, perfectly clear. Congratulations, Jordan. You don't over-look the smallest detail, do you? No wonder you've achieved so much in your life. However, what you're trying to achieve now is ridiculous. Nobody makes demands like the ones you've made—not if they've any sense!'

'Then you know what to do, don't you? Nobody is

forcing you to accept my offer, Katherine. It's entirely up to you at the end of the day.' He shrugged lightly enough, but she could see the rim of colour which edged his angular cheekbones and the hard glitter which shone in his eyes as he looked at her. Jordan was furious at the way she had spoken to him, but suddenly she didn't care.

'Yes, it is up to me, as you say. However, have you stopped to think what it will mean for you when it gets out that you refused to help your own wife's brother?' She gave a taunting laugh. 'I'm sure it won't look good once the papers get hold of the story.'

'If that is a threat then I would think very carefully before going ahead with it.' His tone was deadly calm, yet it vibrated with a note which made a shiver run through her when she heard it. 'I'm sure that the papers would be equally interested to learn what happened eighteen months ago, when I agreed to bail your father out. Are you sure you would like that story to be plastered all over the tabloids as well?'

He shrugged as he turned to walk to the door. 'It could be very distressing for Adam to have all those details raked up, I imagine.'

'You…you wouldn't do that!' she cried, horrified by the thought.

He glanced back at her, his face hard and set. 'I wouldn't do it out of choice, but if you push me too hard, Katherine, then believe me, I would.'

She swallowed hard, feeling the fear knotting deep in her stomach. She had never meant the conversation to deteriorate like this, not when she wanted to convince Jordan to see the situation from her point of view. She looked down at the floor, realising that she had gone about this in entirely the wrong way. She had to convince Jordan to see sense by staying calm rather than by trying to…to threaten him!

'If you could just lend Peter the money he needs then I'm sure he will pay you back. It might take him some time…'

Jordan gave a deep laugh which stopped her dead. 'Oh, you're right there, Katherine. It would take Peter a very long time to repay me. And once interest started accruing on top then we'd be talking years. I'm afraid I'm not prepared to wait that long.'

'Interest? You'd charge Peter interest on the loan?' Her voice reflected her shock, but Jordan merely shrugged.

'Naturally. After all I do have a business to run, and my money can be put to a lot better use than saving your brother's miserable skin.' He paused as though to let what he was saying sink in. 'However, it is entirely up to you if Peter has to spend the rest of his life with that debt hanging around his neck.'

'Why me?' Jordan had already opened the door, and she saw him stop. She took a step towards him, her grey eyes heavy with anguish as they searched his face. 'If a child means so much to you, Jordan, then I won't put any obstacles in your way if you want to…to divorce me.'

His laughter was harsh, yet it held something other than anger—pain, regret, a bitterness which somehow made her ache just to hear it. Katherine had no idea which, and gave up trying to understand as Jordan continued in a tone so hard that each word made her flinch.

'I shall never divorce you, Katherine! Understand that right away. I swore before God to take you as my wife until death, and I never break my word once I have given it. I don't see marriage as something to be discarded at the drop of a hat, so if I do have a child then it will be the child you give me—otherwise there won't be one. It's as simple as that.'

Katherine stared at him in horror as she tried to absorb what he was telling her, but it was just too much to take in. She closed her eyes in despair while she tried to tell herself that it was simply another ploy to get what he wanted, that he didn't really mean it, but she knew deep down that he did.

Jordan would deny himself the child he wanted if she refused to give it to him. It put an almost intolerable pressure upon her.

'That isn't fair, Jordan.' Her voice was hoarse, her face like wax as she opened her eyes and stared at him. 'It isn't fair to tell me that!'

'Maybe it isn't, but then very little in life is ever fair. At some point each and every one of us has to do what he feels is right for himself, no matter what the repercussions are for those around us. Peter chose his path when he gambled away that money. He didn't give much thought to anyone else, did he? You have the right to make the same choice and leave him to sort out the mess he's made by himself.'

Katherine felt her temper roar to life at his refusal to see things in any other way than the way that suited him. She welcomed it because it felt so much better than this soul-destroying numbness. 'Maybe you can turn your back on someone who needs help but I can't!' She gave a scornful laugh, wanting to hit back at him in some way, to put a dent in his composure, and suddenly she knew the best way to do it.

'God knows, I didn't have much of an opinion of you before, but after what you told me last night... Well! Frankly, the thought of any child of mine having your genes disgusts me! I shall find the money Peter needs without your help, thank you very much. Even selling myself on the streets appeals more than what you are asking in return!'

He went so still that for a moment Katherine fancied he'd stopped breathing. She knew that her own breath had locked deep in her chest because her lungs were aching with the pressure. For a moment that seemed to verge on eternity he just stood and looked at her, and then he wrenched at the door and walked away.

Katherine gave a broken sob as the air forced itself out of her body at last. She was trembling so hard that it seemed impossible to take another breath. She closed her eyes and saw Jordan's face, the expression in his eyes for that second before he walked away. She didn't think she would ever forget it, or forgive herself for putting it there.

It was late afternoon when Katherine arrived at the towering office block which housed the headquarters of J.J. Engineering. Where the day had gone since Jordan had walked out of the flat that morning she had no idea. She had spent hours just staring blankly at the wall while she remembered everything they had said to one another, the way Jordan had looked before he left...

A shudder ran through her before she straightened her shoulders and walked through the glass doors. J.J. Engineering had its offices on the top two floors of the building so Katherine took the lift, her heart thundering as she ran through what she was going to say to Jordan. Whether he would be prepared to accept her apology or not was another matter.

Her eyes swam with sudden tears as the lift stopped. She made her way along the corridor towards Jordan's office, then stopped to get a handkerchief out of her bag and wipe her eyes. She was vaguely aware of someone coming along the corridor behind her but she didn't look round, not wanting anyone to see how upset she was.

'Katherine? I thought it was you. What a lovely surprise... Good heavens, what's wrong?'

Charles sounded alarmed as he saw her tears. He bent towards her, his face full of concern. 'What's happened, Katherine? You're not feeling ill, are you?'

Katherine tried to smile, but it was impossible now that the floodgates had opened and tears were streaming down her face. She didn't demur when Charles urged her into his office and closed the door. He seemed at a loss to know what to do as he patted her arm.

'There, there, my dear. Surely it can't be that bad?'

Katherine sniffed as she mopped her eyes. 'I'm so sorry, Charles. It's really inexcusable of me. It's just that Jordan and I—' Her voice broke as another sob racked her.

Charles's mouth tightened. He drew her into his arms, his hand shaking as he stroked her hair. 'I might have known Jordan was behind this! He really is a first-rate bastard. I don't know why the hell you stay with him, Katherine!'

He drew back to stare into her face, and she was startled to see the anger in his usually mild brown eyes. 'Leave him, Katherine! God knows, you aren't happy with him; it doesn't take much to work that out. Tell him that you're leaving him and come away with me.'

'Charles...'

Charles didn't appear to notice her shock. His eyes were blazing now, his face suffused with sudden colour. 'I love you, Katherine! You must know that. All I want is for you to be happy, and we could be. You and I could be so happy together!'

'Charles…please!' Katherine stared at him aghast. 'Please, you're making a dreadful mistake…'

Charles laughed harshly as he drew her to him and held her so close that Katherine could barely move. 'The only mistake I've made is not telling you how I feel sooner! I should have made you leave Jordan months ago instead of allowing you to be subjected to his abominable behaviour!'

'No! Charles…no! You've got this all wrong…' Katherine got no further as Charles's mouth covered hers. She twisted her head to try and escape him, scarcely able to believe what was happening, that this was Charles—kind, gentle Charles—doing this!

She gave a sharp little moan as she felt his teeth graze her bottom lip, then gasped as he was suddenly wrenched away from her and went spinning across the room to land in a heap against the wall. She raised a shaking hand to her mouth, trembling with shock at what had happened and the speed with which the situation had been resolved.

'Clear your desk and be out of here within the next ten minutes. Oh, and make sure that you don't forget anything because you won't be coming back!'

Jordan's voice grated with a depth of fury Katherine had never heard before in anyone's voice. She shot a horrified look at him, but he wasn't looking at her. His gaze was focused on Charles, who was struggling to his feet. The violence which emanated from Jordan right then terrified her, because she wasn't sure what would happen if he lost control. Somehow she had to defuse the situation if she could.

'Jordan, I…'

His eyes blazed as he swung round. 'Go to my office and stay there, Katherine.' He gave a sharp downward thrust of his hand as she opened her mouth. 'Don't say anything. Just do it—if you want your ''friend'' to walk away and not be carried out of here on a stretcher! Believe me, I'm only waiting for the excuse.'

Katherine shot one last look at Charles, then turned and fled from the room, shocked by the bitterness she'd heard in Jordan's voice. Did he blame her for what had happened? Did he imagine that she had encouraged Charles to behave the way he had? Her desire to get right away from the situation was so great that she was tempted to flee from the building. Only the thought of what Jordan might do to Charles if he found she had gone stopped her.

The door to Jordan's office was open so Katherine went inside. She walked over to the window and stared blindly down to the street while she wondered what was happening, if…if Jordan had managed to hold onto his control. He had been so angry…!

She swung round as she heard the door close, the colour ebbing and flowing in her face as her heart raced unsteadily. Jordan didn't say anything as he stood and looked at her. His face was hard and set, his blue eyes so dark that they almost appeared black.

Suddenly he strode across the room and disappeared into the bathroom; Katherine heard water running. When he came out again, she could see that he was carrying a towel, one end of which had been soaked in water.

He came straight over to her, his face expressionless as he lifted her chin and gently applied the cold, wet towel to her cut lip. Katherine flinched at the contact and felt his fingers contract although he never uttered a word. He just continued to dab at the cut before gently running the moistened cloth around her whole mouth, as though by doing so he could wipe away the evidence of what had happened, the way Charles had kissed her…

'I should have killed him when I had the chance.' His voice was so low that she had to strain to hear it, yet its calmness wasn't a reflection of how he was feeling. Katherine could see the fury in his blue eyes as they lifted to hers, just as she could see it in the way his big hand clenched on the towel.

Her eyes filled with tears again, so that his face swam. 'I'm sorry, Jordan,' she whispered brokenly. 'I never wanted that to happen. I had no idea that Charles…that he…'

A sob shuddered through her and she heard Jordan curse roughly as he tossed the towel onto his desk and then drew her into his arms. 'Shh, it's all right. Don't cry, Katherine.'

His hand was so gentle as he brushed the damp blonde hair back from her wet face, so tender—and yet she recalled the violence in him just moments before. She looked up in shock and saw his mouth thin as he understood. 'I may be a bastard of the first order but I would never lift a finger against you, Katherine!'

'I know that.' She felt a ripple of surprise run through her as she realised it was true. Her eyes lifted to his. She was faintly puzzled by the discovery. 'I've never been afraid of you in that way, Jordan.'

He smiled very gently, and it seemed to her that some of the violence seeped from him at the soft confession. 'Good. I should hate to think that you were afraid of me.' He held her for a moment more, then let her go so abruptly that she wondered if there was something wrong. However, all he did was retrieve the towel from the desk and take it back to the bathroom to wet it again. He came back and handed it to her.

'Your lip is starting to swell up. You'd better keep that on it for a while.'

Katherine's face flamed as she took the towel then went and sat down on a chair—her legs had begun to tremble. Jordan watched her for a moment, then went over to his desk and rang through to his secretary. 'Cancel the rest of my appointments for today, Dorothy, please. See if you can reschedule anything urgent for the morning. And while you're at it get on to Mr Langtree's secretary and warn her that he has had to leave.'

He paused as the woman queried the instruction, his gaze drifting to Katherine and remaining on her as he added softly, 'I'm afraid Mr Langtree won't be coming in tomorrow, or any other day for that matter. He is no longer working for the company. I shall take over anything urgent he was dealing with for now.'

He ended the call, his face giving little away as to how he felt about the stir this was going to cause. Katherine couldn't begin to speculate on what his secretary thought. It would be all round the building before the day was out—the fact that Charles had left so abruptly…the reason why he had done so!

'Nobody has any idea why he left and they won't find out. Charles will be left in no doubt of what will happen should he consider talking about that unsavoury incident.'

Jordan had guessed what she was thinking with such ease that she felt stunned. She turned a white face towards him. 'It's all my fault, Jordan, isn't it? I should never have encouraged him.' She stammered a little as she realised how that might be interpreted. 'Oh, I…I don't mean that I encouraged him in that way! What I mean is that I should never have allowed him to become so friendly that he started misinterpreting it. Now Charles is out of a job, you've lost a valuable employee, and it's all my fault!'

'I'd say the fault lies with both of us, Katherine,' he replied, somewhat obliquely. 'As for Charles being out of a job, well, I shall make certain that he receives a handsome pay-off in return for his discretion. And, as for losing a valuable employee, I'm afraid that isn't quite true. Charles has had difficulty in keeping up with the demands of the job for some time now. Maybe it's better that he goes now.'

Was Jordan just saying that to make her feel better? She got to her feet a little unsteadily and managed a shaky smile. 'Well, I'm sorry that I ruined your day. I didn't come here for that.'

'Why did you come?' He came around the desk and sat down on the corner of it.

Katherine smoothed a hand down her dress to iron out a non-existent wrinkle while she gave herself time to think. The nice little speech she had prepared so carefully had suddenly flown out of her head, and was it any wonder?

'Katherine? Tell me, sweetheart.'

His voice was warm enough to make it suddenly easier, so she just said what she wanted to without any adornment. 'I came to apologise for the horrible things I said before. I regretted them almost immediately. I…I wanted to hurt you, Jordan, that's why I said them, but it was a dreadful thing to do.'

He shrugged as he stood up. 'Not if it was how you felt. Forget it, Katherine…'

'No! I can't forget it.' She moved towards him, her eyes imploring him to understand. 'And it isn't how I feel. You…you would be the sort of father any child would be proud of, Jordan!'

He went utterly still, and then he gave a deep sigh which held a hint of weariness. 'But would I be the sort of father *you* want for your children, Katherine? That's the real crux of the matter, isn't it?'

His eyes bored into hers before he suddenly smiled. 'But I have no intention of putting you on the spot by demanding that you answer that right now, not after what's happened. I'm not that crass.'

He glanced at his watch, then looked back at her with a lift of his brows. 'What do you say that we go out for an early dinner and then see if we can find tickets for a show? Although I can't promise you the best seats in the house at this late stage. I think we could both do with a little light relief after what's happened, don't you?'

'Oh…' Katherine didn't know what to say. They never went out together, unless it was to some sort of function where questions would be asked if they didn't both turn up. This was a totally new departure, and she wasn't sure what to think.

'I'm not really dressed…' she began, cautiously.

Jordan laughed. 'How like a woman! You look beautiful. But you would look beautiful wearing a plastic bin-liner!' He caught her by the shoulders and swiftly propelled her towards the bathroom. 'Go in there and fuss a little if it makes you feel better, although to my way of thinking it's not necessary.'

Katherine still hesitated. 'We still need to discuss what you're going to do about Peter.'

His face hardened once more. 'I've told you what I want, Katherine, and that won't change. However, you need time to make up your mind. I don't want you rushing into a decision and regretting it.'

'But we don't have time. Those people are already pressing Peter for the money!'

Jordan drew himself up, looking big and arrogant as he stood there and stared at her. 'I have made it very clear to your brother's creditors how displeased I would be if they did anything rash. They have agreed to wait until Peter is back from his honeymoon. And believe me, Katherine, nobody is going to be foolish enough to start making waves now that I am involved. Now, go and get ready. You don't need to worry about telling me your answer tonight, that's for sure!'

He walked back to his desk and picked up a file. Katherine studied his down-bent head then slowly went into the small bathroom. She stared at her reflection in the mirror and saw the surprise in her eyes, the uncertainty. The more she learned about Jordan the less, she realised, she knew about him!

CHAPTER EIGHT

KATHERINE and Jordan had dinner at a small Italian restaurant, tucked away down a side street, well away from the bustle of the evening commuter traffic. There were few other diners there so early, and they had the place almost to themselves.

'I hope you like Italian food.' Jordan smiled as he handed her the menu, his blue eyes gleaming with laughter. 'I never thought to ask!'

Katherine felt the colour seep under her skin as she understood the reason for his amusement. They had been married a year yet they still knew so little about one another's tastes!

She put the menu down on the red and white checked cloth because her hand was shaking. 'Italian food is one of my favourites, as it happens. What do you recommend, seeing as you have been here before?' she said as levelly as she could manage.

'Mmm, let me see.' He treated her to another lingering smile then turned his attention to the menu. The waiter had lit the candle in the centre of the table when they sat down, even though it was still too light outside to warrant it. Now the soft shimmer given off by its flame gleamed on Jordan's dark hair, turning it to black satin.

Katherine felt her mouth go dry as she wondered how it would feel, how different it would be from the hair on the rest of his body which was so crisp...

'Linguini with sweet basil and tomato sauce.' He

111

looked up suddenly and frowned as he caught her expression. 'Are you all right?'

'I... Er, yes, of course.' She cleared her throat and concentrated on the menu, but the letters swirled in front of her so that she couldn't spot the dish he had recommended until a tanned finger landed on the page to point it out.

'Oh, I see. Thank you.' Her voice sounded as though it had been put through a wringer, it was so thin and tight as it issued from her throat. She stared down at her hands, knowing that if Jordan mocked her nervousness right then she would simply shrivel up.

'Shall I order for both of us, then? I'm sure you won't be disappointed. And how about some Chianti Classico to go with it? That would be perfect. Not that I claim to be any sort of wine buff. I'm afraid my palate isn't as educated as it should be, but I know what I like, and that seems the best way of choosing wine by my way of thinking.'

Katherine felt a rush of gratitude at the way he hadn't tried to take advantage of the moment, as he could have done. She smiled at him with genuine warmth as she looked up. 'Whatever you choose will be fine, Jordan.'

Just for a second his eyes blazed, before he carefully banked down the fires, but she knew they were still there all the same. She took a sip of water and felt shaken by the fact that she had never before noticed the way Jordan looked at her with such hunger. Had it only started in the past few days or had it been going on for longer than that? Had she deliberately avoided seeing it? She wasn't sure, but what she *was* sure of was that seeing his desire now didn't shock her so much as exhilarate her, and that was a far more dangerous reaction in her estimation.

Passion was the greediest of all emotions because it

could take a person over completely. She had seen it happen, had seen the way her mother had been ruled by passion, and had always been afraid that it might happen to her, that she might have inherited that flaw in Caroline's character as she had inherited so many of her mother's other characteristics.

If she allowed herself to be swept away by this passion for Jordan which she knew simmered just below the surface then she might never be able to free herself from its clutches. She might find herself driven by the need to feed it—with this man...or another!

'I have the feeling that I was conned. Completely and utterly taken for a ride!'

Jordan laughed ruefully as he glanced at her. Katherine laughed with him, enjoying the fact that he could see the funny side of what had happened.

'You weren't to know the seats would be up in the gods, Jordan. Although that ticket tout did promise that we would have a heavenly view of the show.'

She dissolved into peals of laughter as she saw his face. He caught her hand and swung her out of the way as another group of theatregoers tried to pass then on the narrow pavement.

'Wretch! One hundred pounds as well...!' He laughed deeply as he started along the street, seemingly unaware that he was still holding her hand. 'Still, I enjoyed the show, despite the fact that all the actors looked like ants because they were so far away. I mean, the music made up for it, didn't it? We got the full benefit of that!'

Katherine giggled. 'We definitely did. My ears are still ringing. I didn't know that they were allowed to put seats that close to the speakers, did you?' she asked with mock innocence.

'Why you…!' He swung her round in front of him, taking hold of her other hand as he held her there. He seemed oblivious to the crowds making their way past them, oblivious to everything apart from her laughing face. Katherine felt her smile falter as she saw the warmth in his eyes, the way he was looking at her so intently…

He gave a sudden deep laugh which broke the spell. 'Next time, young lady, I shall leave *you* to make the arrangements. Let's see how well you fare, shall we?'

He let go of one of her hands, although he still retained his hold on the other as he started walking again. Katherine kept pace with him, feeling the constriction in her chest ease a little, although the confusion she felt was growing as the night passed.

Jordan wasn't blind, he could see how aware of him she was, yet he wasn't making any attempt to use it to his advantage. Why? What was he up to? Or wasn't he up to anything apart from enjoying the evening? As she was…

She shot him a quick glance from under her lashes, and saw the smile which still played around his beautiful mouth. There was a light breeze blowing, and it ruffled his hair and plastered the thin white shirt to his chest as his jacket blew open. Katherine felt a quiver race up her spine as she remembered how his body had looked naked…

She took a quick little breath to rid herself of the memory and looked round, suddenly realising that Jordan was heading down to the Embankment. 'Why are we going down here?'

'It's too nice a night to rush home. Let's take a walk along by the river.' He glanced at her bare arms, then let go of her hand to slip off his jacket and drape it around her shoulders. 'Here, I don't want you catching a chill.'

'You need this more than I do. Don't forget how ill you've been, Jordan.' She tried to give it back to him but he wouldn't let her. He drew the lapels together across her chest so that she was cocooned in the soft wool which still bore the heat and scent of his body. Katherine felt her senses stir as she felt Jordan's warmth stealing into her, smelled the scent of his skin surrounding her.

'Keep it on, Katherine. I'm fine.' His voice dropped a note. It was dark and vibrant as he added in a soft undertone she wasn't sure she was meant to hear, 'I can't remember feeling this good, in fact.'

There seemed nothing she could say without making too much out of a situation which was already more fraught than it should be. When Jordan started walking again, Katherine followed him. She looked round, searching for something to say to take the edge off all the raw emotions which seemed to fill the night with danger. One unwary word could catapult them into a situation she might only regret.

'I used to love coming here when I was a child,' she said carefully, her tone slightly stilted. 'Daddy used to come to the House of Lords when there was something being debated he was particularly interested in. Peter and I would stay at the flat with our nanny, and, if he got back early enough, Daddy would come home and collect us then take us for a walk down by the river.'

'I keep forgetting that your father has a title. He never uses it, does he?'

Katherine shrugged. 'He doesn't see any point. In his view it's simply something he has inherited rather than earned for himself. The only time he has ever taken advantage of it, in fact, was to take his seat in the Lords. Peter and I used to look forward to those occasions, I can tell you!'

Jordan laughed softly. 'It sounds as though those times are full of pleasant memories, Katherine.'

'They are. I shall never forget them, I don't think. But then I suppose your childhood is always special, isn't it…?' She stopped, aghast, as she realised what she had said. 'I'm sorry, Jordan. That was incredibly insensitive of me.'

'Not at all. I enjoyed you sharing it with me.' He stopped as they came to one of the street-lamps, and he turned to look at her. 'My lack of happy memories doesn't mean you shouldn't enjoy yours. Every child should have the chance to build up a store of good memories to look back on.'

'As…as you want your child to do?'

The words slid out before she could stop them. They hung between them, sweetly poignant in the circumstances. Jordan's child, if he had one, would be her child too. Both of them would give that child the memories which were so important. All three lives would be intrinsically entwined from the moment of the child's birth.

Katherine started walking again, aware on one level of consciousness that Jordan was now keeping pace with her. Her mind was racing almost as fast as her feet were moving, thoughts flying in and out of her head so fast that she could grasp only a few of them.

Her child. Jordan's child. With blond hair and blue eyes, or black hair and grey. The combinations were endless. Parts of her and Jordan would make a blueprint for another human being who in time might produce another…

'Katherine.' His voice claimed her attention at last, and she stopped, aware that her breath was coming in laboured spurts. She hardly dared look at him because he must know how she felt. He must feel the same way... Her eyes lifted to his, heavy with confusion and uncertainty.

'Don't!' Jordan touched her face lightly, almost despairingly. 'Don't think about it if it causes you such distress.' He glanced over his shoulder, missing her shocked gasp. 'We'd better go back. It's late and I have a few things to sort out.'

He took her arm as he led her back the way they had come. They passed another couple—arms locked around one another's waists, lost in a world of their own. The comparison to the way she and Jordan were walking along—his hand politely cupping her elbow—was too sharp. Katherine felt it sting her temper to life with a speed that shocked her.

'It wouldn't work, Jordan!'

He didn't pretend not to understand. 'Why not? We've proved tonight that it's possible for us to spend a few hours together in a fair degree of harmony—even, dare I say, enjoy being together? Why couldn't we live together and raise a child, give it the love and security it needs?' His voice dropped, achingly tender all of a sudden. 'Why can't we give that child a lifetime's worth of wonderful memories?'

He was so persuasive! Even though she knew it was crazy, Katherine could feel the temptation to accede to his demands. A child to love and care for, to watch over while it grew. She had never allowed herself to think about it before, yet in the past three days the thought had been constantly at the back of her mind.

Katherine knew in her own heart how much she would

love having a child, how it would fulfil a deep need in her she had been barely aware of before. But it was the way that child would arrive into the world which scared her, the way it would be conceived!

'No!' She gave a sharp laugh which carried along the path so that the other couple looked round. She moderated her tone—tried her hardest to moderate how she was feeling. It had been so easy in the past to keep a rein on her emotions, but it was so difficult around Jordan lately!

'You have to see how mad the idea is. Children are astute, and they soon see through any pretence. How long would it take for a child to realise that something was wrong, that you and I didn't...didn't love one another?'

His lids flickered down, hiding his eyes from her. 'Is love necessary? Perhaps the most essential thing of all between two people is respect. I respect you, Katherine. I hope that you at least feel that for me.'

'I don't know how you can say what you feel!' She reacted to the question instinctively, afraid to let herself think too deeply about how she felt. 'Face it, Jordan, we might be married but we hardly know anything about one another, do we?'

He gave a deep laugh as he took her arm again and led her back onto the road. Katherine had the impression that he was amused by what she had said, but she couldn't understand why. 'I think we know a lot more than you imagine, Katherine, but you're right. We do need to know more. I've been thinking that myself only tonight, and there is a very easy solution.'

He hailed a passing taxi and opened the door for her to get in. Katherine had to wait until he had given the address to the driver before asking the question. 'What sort of solution? What do you mean?'

'That we get to know one another better, of course.' The light from the street-lamps flickered across his face, making it difficult for her to see his expression clearly. 'We've been married a year, so it's about time we made some sort of effort. And if you're ever to reach a decision then surely you need to know exactly what you might be letting yourself in for? Or turning down?'

Katherine didn't know what to say. She had wanted to talk to Jordan about this calmly and rationally for the best part of the day, and now that was just what he was doing—having a perfectly calm, completely rational conversation, albeit a little one-sided. The trouble was that the view Jordan was expressing wasn't quite what she'd had in mind.

She sat in silence throughout the rest of the short journey, unsure whether she was glad or sorry when the taxi drew up outside the flat. Jordan helped her out of the cab then leaned through the window to speak to the driver. Katherine let herself into the entrance hall of the flats and made her way to the lift, her mind going over what Jordan had said.

'Katherine, wait a moment. I'll say goodnight here rather than come all the way up with you.'

She came to an abrupt halt, her face mirroring confusion. 'I'm sorry? What do you mean, you'll say goodnight here?'

He shrugged lightly, his shoulders straining the thin cotton shirt. 'I won't be staying here tonight—nor tomorrow night, for that matter.'

She wet her dry lips. 'Then...then where will you be staying? I don't understand.'

'I'll go to my club. There'll be no problem about them

finding me a room, even at this hour of the night. As to why I won't be staying here, well, a couple of reasons spring to mind. First off, I think we both need a little breathing space right at the moment. What you said before is true—we don't know one another very well. And the reason for that is that we never took the time to do so before we got married.' He smiled. 'In all honesty, it didn't seem necessary, did it? We knew why we were marrying and that was enough. Now things have changed.'

She wanted to deny it but couldn't. She felt her heart bump painfully as Jordan took a step towards her, and she wondered wildly if he was going to kiss her goodnight. But would she let him?

'Do you mind if I take my jacket? You shouldn't be cold now that you're inside.'

His voice was warm honey, smooth and sweet with awareness. Katherine knew with absolute certainty that he had guessed what had been racing through her head just now! She slid the jacket off her shoulders and handed it to him with a stiff little murmur of thanks which he acknowledged with another of those infuriating smiles.

'Thank you. I must say that I have enjoyed this evening. I shall look forward to tomorrow all the more.' He flipped the jacket over his shoulder, hooking it on the end of a finger. 'I'll pick you up around twelve-thirty, OK?'

He had already started to leave before she found her voice. 'Wait! What do you mean? Where are you taking me?'

He grinned, looking so boyishly handsome as he stood there playing games with her that she wanted to scream.

'On a picnic. Let's hope it's a nice day. It should be fun.'

'Picnic...! But why? Jordan, what is this all about—?'

'It's simple. I am going to court you, Katherine. All right, so it's a little like putting the cart before the horse, having the wedding before the courtship, but who's going to argue? As to why I'm going to do so—well, if you try I'm sure you can work that out easily enough. Be ready at twelve-thirty. Sleep tight.'

He made it to the door this time before she managed to get her brain into gear. But the question which came out wasn't the one she had meant to ask. There seemed to be some sort of a log-jam in her mind—questions were piling up one on top of the other, and this one broke through first.

'You said that was the first reason for your not staying tonight. What other reason do you have?'

He stared down at the floor for a moment before he turned to look at her, and his voice was suddenly raw with a hunger he made no attempt to hide. 'Because I don't trust myself to be in the flat with you and not break my promise, Katherine. That's why!'

He was gone before she had time to draw breath, the clatter of the door swinging back and forth on its hinges echoing in the silence. She turned and blindly made her way up to the flat, then went to the window. The taxi was just turning out of the driveway, she could see its red tail-lights glowing as the driver braked. Red for danger, she thought wildly. Red as a warning.

She only hoped she could heed it, but she was less sure than ever that she could after tonight.

If Jordan had stayed then *would* she have resisted if he had tried to make love to her?

CHAPTER NINE

IT WAS twelve-thirty on the dot when the doorbell rang. Katherine shot a glance in the mirror, suddenly wishing she had worn something else. Were jeans and a sleeveless top really suitable? And should she have left her hair loose when it made her look so…so young?

She turned away from her reflection as the bell rang a second time, realising that she was focusing on such trivialities to avoid thinking about the real issue. Jordan had stated quite clearly what he intended last night—he intended to court her. The idea should have been ridiculous in the circumstances, yet she found herself unable to dismiss it as such. Jordan had an uncanny knack of getting what he wanted when he set his mind to it!

He gave her a slow smile as she opened the door, his blue eyes dancing with laughter as they swept over her. 'Two minds with but one thought, Katherine?' He looked meaningfully at her denim jeans and white top, an almost identical outfit to the one he was wearing.

Katherine coloured, but she didn't rise to the challenge. Odd that they should have both chosen to wear much the same thing…

Her gaze swept from the top of his gleaming dark head to his short-sleeved white T-shirt. The thin fabric clung to his torso, outlining the muscles which rippled across his back as he moved away. Her gaze ran lower, over the well-washed denim which emphasised the taut curve of his buttocks, the powerful length of his legs…

She took a deep breath to dispel the sudden dizziness,

but her voice was faintly husky when she spoke. 'I…I'll just get a sweater.'

He looked round, seemingly just becoming aware that she was still standing by the front door. His eyes searched hers, and Katherine had the distinct impression that he was pleased by what he saw.

She hurried to her room, not even allowing herself to speculate on what he might have seen on her face. How she was going to get through the next few hours she had no idea! She had lain awake half the night worrying about it. Now she realised that she should have rung Jordan and simply cancelled their arrangements. In fact, it wasn't too late to do that even now!

She swung round to go back and tell him that, then stopped as she saw that he had followed her in and was lounging in the doorway. He let his gaze travel around the room before he gave a soft whistle.

'Did you have a little trouble deciding what to wear today, Katherine? Or are you donating all this to a jumble sale?'

Katherine followed his gaze, and bit her lip as she saw the state the room was in. The bed was heaped with discarded clothing, the doors of the wardrobe hanging open to show row after row of bare hangers. She had put on and taken off one outfit after another, not finding anything she considered suitable. But why had it been so difficult to choose something? Because…because she had wanted to look her best for Jordan?

The answer was too uncomfortably close to the truth to be palatable. Katherine cleared her throat. 'Ahem…I was just…just sorting through my wardrobe to see what needs sending to the cleaner's. Now shall we go?'

'I'm ready whenever you are.' Jordan didn't move as she started towards him. 'Don't forget your sweater,

Katherine. That's if you don't intend sending it to the cleaner's along with all the rest of this stuff.'

He headed out of the room, leaving Katherine fuming. She found a soft cream wool sweater in a drawer and shrugged it around her shoulders.

Jordan was waiting for her by the front door. Katherine stole a glance at him, seeing the faint smile which still curved his lips, and bit back a sigh. She must be mad to go with him today, but then hadn't she been acting crazily ever since he had turned up at the church? One minute her life had been flowing along its usual orderly path, and the next... Well!

The sun was hot as they stepped out of the building. Katherine slipped off her sweater and glanced round with a frown. 'Where's your car?'

'Here.' Jordan led her over to where a small open-topped sports car was parked.

Katherine stared at its gleaming deep purple body-work in surprise. 'But this isn't the car you usually drive?'

'It most definitely isn't. In fact, today is a sort of celebration, Katherine. It's taken me the best part of two years to restore this car, and today is its first official outing.' He opened the passenger door and bowed. 'Would my lady care to be my first passenger?'

Katherine slid into the seat, astounded by what he had told her. She looked up as he closed the door, her eyes mirroring her surprise. 'I had no idea you enjoyed that sort of thing, Jordan.'

The amusement faded from his face abruptly, to be replaced by a weary cynicism. 'I'm sure you hadn't, but then there is an awful lot you don't know about me, Katherine.'

Katherine felt a shiver run through her at the note in

his voice. She stared through the windscreen as Jordan slid behind the wheel and turned the key in the ignition, knowing in her heart that he was right—there *was* such a lot she didn't know about him. The Jordan James she'd thought she knew—the hard, cold businessman—was just one facet of him. It was a side she understood and could deal with, but this other side he had started to show her recently was very different. She wasn't sure she could deal with this new Jordan nearly so effectively!

'You don't mind the hood being down, do you? It is a glorious day.'

Jordan had to raise his voice over the throbbing of the engine. Katherine took a quick breath and fought to control the fear which was seeping through her. Jordan could only affect her if she allowed him to; she had to remember that.

'No, of course I don't mind.' She held back her hair as the wind whipped it across her face, and fixed a determinedly bright smile to her mouth. 'It would be a shame not to have the top off. There can't be many days when that's possible in England.'

Jordan laughed as he eased the car through a gap in the traffic. 'Too right! I can't believe how fortunate we are with the weather today.' He shot her a quick glance, his eyes burning with something she found difficult to understand. 'I wanted today to be special, Katherine, and it seems even the weather is working in my favour.'

She didn't ask him what he meant because she wasn't sure she wanted to know. Jordan had told her that he wanted them to get to know one another better, but the thought scared her. Was it wise to learn more about him? What she had discovered recently had thrown her into such confusion...

She searched for something to ease the suddenly tense silence. 'What sort of car is this? I'm afraid I don't know anything at all about cars.'

His lips curled into a smile which showed he understood what she was trying to do, but he followed her lead. 'An E-type Jaguar. It's well over twenty years old, and when I found it in a breaker's yard it was a complete wreck. It took a hell of a lot of work to restore it, but it's worth it, wouldn't you say?'

Katherine smiled her agreement, feeling a little more at ease because he had accepted her lead. 'It's beautiful. I don't recall ever seeing one like it before except in old pictures.'

'Don't! Do you have to rub it in how much older I am than you? I used to spend hours dreaming about owning one of these cars when I was a kid, and here you are calmly informing me that you don't even remember seeing any on the roads!'

Katherine couldn't help laughing at his wry admission. 'Sorry, but you are ten years older than me, Jordan,' she teased.

'Mmm, and double that in experience. Think that's an obstacle, Katherine? The fact that I have done and seen so much that you can't even begin to comprehend? We come from different worlds, don't we? I doubt you really understand what made me into the man I am today.' He paused deliberately and she felt her heart still as she waited to hear what else he would say. 'And I can't really understand what made you into the woman you are unless you open up and tell me.'

Katherine didn't know what to say, because what Jordan was asking her to do was something she couldn't bear to think about. How could she ever tell him all those intimate details of her life? How could she tell him about her mother?

She avoided looking at him and heard him sigh. 'I can't do this all by myself. It takes two to make a marriage work.'

'Maybe this marriage was never meant to work. Maybe…maybe you're asking the impossible, Jordan!' Her voice was husky with pain and the shame which had been such a part of her for so long. She saw Jordan's hands tighten on the steering wheel until his knuckles turned white from the pressure.

'I shall make it work, Katherine!' The assertion in his voice made her turn, and she saw the anger which blazed in his eyes as he looked at her. 'I shall make it work because I shall never let you go. Understand?'

Katherine felt a sense of desolation sweep through her as he looked back at the road. Jordan wanted their marriage to work because he refused to break his vows. It was as simple and as complicated as that. He refused to admit that it might become untenable at some point. He couldn't see that it might end up destroying them both!

Jordan parked the car and shut off the engine. They had completed the drive in silence, each of them busy with their own thoughts. Katherine prayed that nothing of what she'd been thinking showed on her face as she felt him studying her now. She felt raw and shaken by their exchange, unable to cope with any more pressure without breaking down.

'I'm sorry.' His voice held a deep contrition which brought her eyes flying to his face. He gave her a thin smile as he reached out to loop a strand of hair behind her ear. His hand rested on her cheek for a moment, warm and strong and oddly comforting. 'Truce,

Katherine? I honestly didn't set out to bombard you the way I did. I'm going too far and too fast, aren't I?'

She shrugged so that his hand fell away. It would be only too easy to let it stay there, but she couldn't indulge in such weakness when one thing could lead to another as…as it had done on their wedding night. All it had taken then was the touch of Jordan's hand…

She quelled the sudden rush of memories, but it seemed harder than ever to relegate them to the back of her mind, so her voice wasn't as steady as she would have liked it to be when she spoke. 'I think you're expecting too much, Jordan. After all, it isn't as though we married for the usual reasons, is it? Maybe it's foolish to try to make changes at this stage. Why not accept what we have and leave it at that? I'm still more than happy to act as your hostess when occasion demands.'

She took a quick breath and made herself continue. 'Any…anything more than that is something you can easily arrange, I imagine.' The idea was oddly unpalatable, even though it had never troubled her before.

His laughter was no more than a ripple, but there was a depth to it which hinted at unseen danger. 'So, I have your permission to take any woman I like to my bed whenever I feel the need? Is that what you're trying to say so delicately, Katherine?'

Her eyes slid away from his, unable to meet the challenge in his stare. 'Yes, I understand why…why you might need that sort of…companionship from time to time. We agreed from the outset that so long as it was done discreetly then there was no reason why it shouldn't be acceptable.'

'And it is perfectly *acceptable* to you? The idea of me making love to some other woman doesn't bother you at all?'

Katherine winced at his bluntness. She forced herself to concentrate on the view to avoid looking at him. Jordan had driven them down to Richmond and parked close to the river; Katherine watched it swirling past, the water glittering in the sunlight, dazzling her eyes to the point where she could no longer see it…

'So I have your permission, do I, to indulge in as many affairs as I want to? To slake my appetites with whoever I please?'

Jordan was goading her to answer, and she turned to glare at him, the dazzle of the water still imprinted on her retinas so that his face was a blur. 'Yes! How many more times do I need to say so?'

Jordan took her face between his hands and bent so that he could look directly into her eyes. 'And how many times do I need to tell you that when I make a promise I keep it?'

Katherine blinked and his face swam back into focus. She felt her breath catch as she saw the expression in his eyes…

'There are no other women? Is that what you're saying?' She swallowed hard, not wanting him to answer, not wanting him to tell her what she knew was true. 'No! I'm sorry, but I don't…'

'I haven't touched another woman since I asked you to marry me, Katherine.'

He let her go and opened the car door to get out. Reaching into the space behind the seats, he lifted out a wicker hamper and balanced it against his hip. 'Ready?'

'Ready…?' Katherine could hear the shock trembling in her voice, as she could feel it running through her. She could barely think, let alone respond. He had made love to no other woman since he had asked her to marry him…?

Her heart lifted. It was simply shock, she told herself, the shock of hearing that a man as virile as Jordan had managed to subdue his needs for such a long time. She wouldn't consider the possibility that she might feel pleased!

'Ready for the picnic, of course. Come on, shake a leg. The champagne is getting warm, and although I might not know much about wine I do know that is a cardinal sin, sweetheart!'

He lifted the basket into his arms and gave her a lazy grin, as though the confession he had just made was of little consequence. Katherine's hand shook as she unlatched the door. She took a steadying breath, terrified that Jordan would guess how unnerved she was, then started violently when she felt his hand slide under her arm as he came round and helped her out. Just for a moment she stared straight into his eyes and saw the awareness written there before she looked away.

Jordan knew how she felt! He understood every one of the emotions which were churning around inside her right then. Had he meant to throw her off-balance by telling her that? Well, if he had, it had been wonderfully effective! Now she must take it as a warning of how far he was prepared to go to achieve his objective.

She moved away from him, not wanting him to feel the shudder which raced through her at the thought of what that objective was!

Katherine picked up the bottle of champagne and drained the last of it into her glass. She glanced at Jordan but he was fast asleep, one arm flung across his eyes to block out the sunlight which was filtering through the boughs of a huge willow tree. She raised the glass to her lips and let some of the wine run down her throat. It was a little warm and flat, but it helped ease the constriction which had stopped her from eating much of the food Jordan had brought.

She glanced at him again, wondering if he really was as relaxed as he seemed to be. But then, she had to allow for the fact that he knew what was going on and she didn't!

She swallowed the rest of the wine then packed the glass into the basket and closed the lid. Her hands were shaking so much that it took her several attempts to slot the wicker peg into its hasp. Jordan had made no more mention of what he had said when he stopped the car, but that didn't mean she had stopped thinking about it. Fat chance of that!

She shot him another wary look, watching a faint frown pucker his brow. What was he thinking about…?

She didn't want to know!

A leaf suddenly dropped off the tree and landed in his hair. Katherine reached over to brush it away and found her fingers lingering. His hair felt cool against her fingertips, as soft as she had imagined it would feel, far softer than the hair on the rest of his body…

Unbidden, her eyes travelled down to where the T-shirt had worked itself loose from the waistband of his jeans. In the gap she could see tanned skin, the line of curling hair which arrowed downwards…

She bit her lip as her heart began to race. She knew how he looked without his clothes on, how that hair arrowed down his body. *She* had seen him naked when no other woman had since they'd been married…

'Katherine…?'

There was a momentary panic in his voice as he suddenly awoke. He sat up so abruptly that she barely had the chance to remove her hand from his hair, and no

chance at all to move away from him. They bumped into
one another, and his hands came up to steady her and
stayed there, holding lightly onto the tops of her bare
arms.

'I…I was just brushing a leaf out of your hair,' she
explained huskily.

'Thank you.' His tone was very grave, but his mouth
curved into a smile which did odd things to her
breathing. Katherine felt goosebumps spring up all over
her skin as he ran his hands lightly down her arms. When
his hands retraced their path, she felt the downy hairs
lift and cling to his fingers as though he had created an
area of static between them. If it had been night, she
thought hazily, they would have seen sparks ignite!

'Are you cold, sweetheart?'

It took a moment for the question to sink in, another
before she could answer it with any degree of normality.
'No…no, of course not. It's warm here.'

'Mmm, it is, yet you're covered in goosebumps.' His
voice was warmer even than the day, gentle amusement
colouring each soft word. He glanced down at her bare
arms then deliberately let his gaze drift to the front of
her thin white top.

Katherine looked down and saw that it wasn't just the
skin on her arms that was reacting to Jordan's touch.
She gave a small gasp of dismay as she saw that her
nipples were thrusting against her cotton blouse in a way
which was little short of brazen!

She twisted out of his hold and scrambled to her feet,
hot and cold flushes playing chase through her blood-
stream. 'Don't you think it's time we started back? We
don't want to get caught up in the rush-hour traffic.'

'There's no hurry. We can always wait until it's over.'

'I…I would prefer to leave now, if you don't mind.'

She bent down to pick up the basket but Jordan caught her hand.

'Stop it, Katherine. It isn't a crime, you know. It's perfectly natural.' He laughed softly. 'And perfectly delightful to my way of thinking!'

'I've no idea what you're talking about. Now, shall I take this or…?'

His hands were suddenly hard as he rose to his feet and held her still. 'I'm talking about the way you responded to me just now.' He glanced down at her aching breasts and his eyes were heavy with knowledge when they came back to hers. 'It is perfectly natural that your body should react that way. It's simply an outward sign of your desire.'

'No! How dare you, Jordan? How dare you imply that I…I…?'

'Want me to touch you there? That, God forbid, you might even want me to make love to you?' His tone was harshly unyielding. 'We are two adults, Katherine. Neither of us should feel shocked that we respond to one another sexually.'

He suddenly drew her to him and held her so that she could feel the way his body had responded even more blatantly than hers. Katherine gave a soft moan as she felt his hardness pressing against her, the way his body pulsed…

'No! I don't want this to happen. I never wanted to feel this way, Jordan! Don't you understand? I can't let myself feel anything like that for you…or…or anyone!'

She pushed him away, then turned and ran back to the car. She half expected him to try to stop her, but when she looked back he was still standing where she had left him, staring across the river. What was he thinking? Was he wondering what she had meant? She crossed her arms across her throbbing breasts and realised that she didn't want to know the answer.

'Would you like to come up for coffee?'

Katherine could hear the stiffness in the invitation and knew that Jordan must hear it too, but she didn't care. She was past pretending, beyond playing games. She just wanted to go inside the flat and try to forget what had happened.

'No, thanks. There are one or two things I need to do.' Jordan's voice sounded just as clipped as hers had been, but Katherine didn't dare speculate on the reason for it.

She got out of the car as fast as she could, then hesitated, unable to bring herself to walk away without saying something.

'Thank you for the drive. I...' She stopped as she found it impossible to utter the lie.

'Don't bother saying how much you enjoyed it, Katherine.' He smiled tightly. There was a nerve beating in his jaw, and the glitter of something hot and dangerous in his eyes which made her blood race as she saw it. 'That would be carrying good manners too far even for you! But some day soon you're going to have to face up to whatever is destroying your life. You can't keep hiding from it. You aren't a frightened child any more, but a woman!'

He slid the car into gear and drove away. Katherine waited until the sound of the engine had faded before turning to go inside. She stopped, suddenly unable to face the thought of spending the night brooding over what had happened—wishing it had been different, wishing even that *she* could be different.

She walked down the drive and on down the street,

letting her feet carry her where they would, letting the thoughts seep from her brain until a merciful emptiness seemed to invade every part of her.

She walked for hours, yet later she couldn't recall where she had been or what she had seen. People passed her by; they all seemed to know where they were going and what they were doing. She didn't. She was no longer in control of her life or her emotions. Maybe she'd never really been in control but had simply had control thrust upon her as it had seemed the only option.

She couldn't change what she was because it was part of her make-up, as intrinsic as the colour of her hair and eyes. She was just like her mother in far too many respects.

It was after midnight when exhaustion finally drove her home. She was trembling with fatigue, so she could barely stand as she summoned the lift. She stood slumped against the wall with her eyes closed as it whisked her upwards. She heard the doors slide open, but it seemed to demand too much effort to move...

'Katherine! Where in the name of God have you been? Look at you!'

Jordan's voice was filled with a mixture of anger and concern. Katherine opened her eyes and looked at him, but she couldn't decide which emotion was uppermost— not that it mattered. She let him lead her into the flat, docile as a lamb as he whisked her into the sitting-room.

'Sit down before you fall down. You have to be the craziest, stupidest, most infuriating...!' He bit off the rest of the less than complimentary tirade as he turned to stride over to the drinks table. Katherine smiled wearily to herself; definitely anger winning, she'd say.

'I don't know what the hell there is to smile about!

I've been going out of my mind here wondering where you'd got to. Drink this.'

He thrust a glass into her hand, then lifted it to her lips when she made no attempt to do anything with it. 'Come on, at least take a couple of sips.'

She pressed her lips together like a mutinous child. 'Don't want it.'

'I don't give a damn what you want! You'll drink it and like it!'

Her temper gave a hiccup as it came to life, then another as it gathered momentum. Katherine glowered back into his angry blue eyes. 'You can't tell me what to do, Jordan! I'm not a child. I am a grown woman quite capable of deciding for myself what I want!'

'Then try acting like one!' His voice grated as he bent towards her and Katherine wondered fancifully if it was possible to smell anger, because she seemed to be able to smell it issuing from Jordan right then—something hot and torrid and darkly disturbing, some scent which made her feel suddenly wonderfully alive after the long hours of numbness. 'Drink it up and do as you're told for once! It will do you good.'

She gave him a taut little smile, watching the way his eyes narrowed as he tried to assess what was behind it. She took the glass out of his hand, then calmly tossed the brandy into his face. 'There—you have it, Jordan. Let's see how much good it does you!'

He shook his head, the brandy running down his face, dripping onto his white T-shirt. Katherine felt a rush of elation as she saw the shock that darkened his eyes. It was about time that Jordan had a taste of his own medicine!

She giggled as she realised how apt the unconscious pun was, but her amusement was quickly curtailed as

Jordan started speaking in a tone which was laced with menace.

'You are going to regret that, sweetheart. Believe me, it was a big mistake!'

Katherine shot to her feet, already regretting the impulse which had led her to do such a thing. She scuttled round the chair as Jordan took a slow step towards her, her breath catching in her throat so that her voice sounded shrill.

'You...you drove me to it, Jordan! It's your fault!'

'Is it indeed? And what if I dispute that?' He took another slow step which brought him so close that Katherine could smell the pungent aroma of the liquor coming off him. She shot a wary glance over her shoulder at the door, another at Jordan's face, then made up her mind.

'Oh, no, you don't!' Jordan's hand snaked out and caught her around the waist before she managed a step. He hauled her back so fast that she slammed against the iron-hard muscles in his chest. He spun her round, his blue eyes blazing almost as hotly as they'd done that night he'd had the fever, only Katherine knew that it was something far more dangerous which caused these flames!

She gave a sudden twist which caught him off-guard and managed to wriggle free, but he was hard on her heels as she fled from the sitting-room. His hand touched her shoulder as she flew into her bedroom, but somehow she slithered away from him. It was only as she turned to close the door that she realised she didn't have a prayer of beating him now. He was simply too strong for her. He was using one hand to hold the door open, smiling arrogantly as he watched her struggle to close it and safely lock him out on the other side!

Katherine could feel the blood beating in her temples as all her pulses raced. She had to do something. She couldn't just give in! She mentally measured the distance to the bathroom. If she could just get inside it…

She whirled round again, but Jordan had already anticipated what she would do. He took two running steps, then hooked his arms around her and neatly brought them both down onto the bed in a tangle of arms and legs. Katherine glared down into his face and spat out her displeasure.

'Let me go, you…you big bully!'

He tightened his grip, obviously taking no chances this time that she might escape. They had landed on top of the jumble of clothes she'd left on the bed, and that had helped cushion their fall, yet Katherine suddenly felt as though all the breath had been knocked out of her body as he eased over onto his back and settled her on top of him.

'Give me one good reason why I should let you go, after what you've just done, Katherine.'

Jordan's voice seemed even deeper than ever. She felt him take a deep breath, as though he too was feeling breathless after their chase. Katherine felt his chest expand upwards and push against her breasts, but it was impossible to ease any space between them with his arms clamped behind her back.

'Because…because it was your fault in the first place,' she muttered a shade thickly.

His black brows rose sharply. 'You're blaming me for your evil temper? Tut, tut—I don't know how you have the gall to stand…' He paused and let his eyes drop meaningfully downwards. 'I should say, to *lie* there and say such a thing.'

Katherine felt the heat sweep up her face as she heard

the nuance in Jordan's voice. Suddenly the air seemed charged, the tension in the room stemming less from anger than a host of other feelings. She wriggled frantically to break his hold on her, then stopped abruptly when Jordan groaned.

'Jordan…are you all right?' Her voice echoed with sudden concern and she saw him smile wryly.

'Never better, and never worse!' A big hand slid down her spine to press her hips against his, and Katherine gasped as she realised what was happening.

Her eyes were huge and softly luminous in the semi-darkness as they flew to his face. There was only the light from the hall filtering into the room, and that was just enough for her to see the expression which crossed his face, more than enough to show her the flames leaping in the depths of his eyes.

'Jordan, I…'

'No.' He touched her mouth with the tip of a finger, his voice gentle and tender. 'Don't. There's no need to be afraid I'll break my promise. There is never any need to be afraid of me, Katherine. If you would only stop being afraid of yourself then maybe this would all be so easy.'

She had no idea what he meant, but it didn't seem to matter all that much as he slid his hand behind her head and drew her down. His mouth was warm and gentle at first, as though he was afraid of scaring her. Katherine tried to hold back the response she could feel beating away inside her, tried to stem the warm wash of sensations which flowed so sweetly through her body, but the kiss broke through her defences. If Jordan had kissed her roughly, taken rather than asked, then maybe she could have denied him… Maybe?

She let herself relax and felt the shudder that ran

through him as her softness melted against him, as her lips stopped trying to evade his and sought them instead. He pulled gently on her hair and raised her head, and his voice was no more than a whisper, so that her name took on the beauty of a prayer as he said it with so much feeling and need. 'Katherine... Katherine...!'

Then he was kissing her again, his mouth hard, urgent, taking and giving at one and the same time, teaching her how to respond, yet seeming to learn from her response. When he felt the shiver which ran through her as he nipped her lower lip, he did it again, even more sensuously, drawing out the moment until she was awash with sensation.

Katherine learned from him too—lessons which were so easy to master. When she felt him stiffen as she ran her fingers through the silky hair at his temples she repeated it, felt him tense again, felt his body shudder beneath hers as though in pain, yet she knew instinctively that it was a very special kind of agony he felt.

He stopped nibbling her lower lip and traced it with his tongue instead, letting it play across the swollen softness until she gasped. Katherine's hands clenched in his hair as she felt his tongue slide inside her mouth and tangle with hers in a rhythm which mimicked the throbbing in the lower part of her body so perfectly. She pushed her hips against his, moving against him as she tried to ease the ache.

'Don't!' Jordan gasped as his hand clenched on her bottom to still her.

He rolled her over with a speed which made her gasp this time, his big body pressing her down into the soft jumble of clothes, the contrast so stark that her senses swam. Softness at her back, such hardness and power pressing down on her...

He took her mouth again in another drugging kiss, then peeled himself away from her and stood up. His eyes blazed as he stared down at her, and his jaw clenched in an effort to keep control of his voice. Yet Katherine could hear the hot swirl of desire in the rough words, the effort it had cost him to stop when he had.

'I won't apologise for what just happened, Katherine,' he grated.

'And I won't ask you to.'

Her reply seemed to stun him almost as much as it stunned her. Katherine saw his hands clench, felt her own do the very same thing. He breathed hard through his nose, his chest rising and falling heavily with each breath. It seemed to take ages before he was able to speak again, although Katherine knew that it was no more than a few seconds in reality. Everything seemed to be suspended at that moment, time hanging in the balance, awaiting their next move...

'I want to stay with you tonight but I won't. I gave you my word that I wouldn't put any pressure on you and I won't break it!'

He turned and strode towards the door, then stopped when she said softly, 'Thank you.'

He glanced round, big and arrogant and...and oddly vulnerable in his aloofness. 'For what? For stopping when what I want most is to make love to you until you scream my name? For being fool enough to let you tie me in knots so that I don't know whether I'm on my head or my heels? What exactly are you thanking me for, Katherine?'

Her eyes shimmered with unshed tears as she heard the ache in his voice. Jordan was a proud man, and that confession must have cost him so much—more than she had a right to expect when she had given him so little in return. Maybe it was that which made her respond truthfully.

'Thank you for caring enough about me to stop when we both know that I wanted you to make love to me…just as much as you wanted to do so.'

He gave a heavy sigh, and his face was suddenly weary. 'You may have wanted it now, Katherine, but what about in the morning, when you woke up? How would you have felt then?' His laughter was bitter. 'I remember how you looked at me the morning after our wedding night, and God knows we stopped before anything really happened! Do you honestly believe that I want to take that sort of risk?'

She felt her heart contract on a spasm of pain and anger and utter confusion. 'Then what do you want from me? Tell me, Jordan!'

'What I *want* is something you probably can't ever give me, Katherine. What I'm willing to settle for is a different matter.'

'I don't understand what you mean…'

He swung the door wide open so that light flooded into the room, yet his face was shadowed because he stood with his back to it, and his voice was oddly flat. 'That at the very least I want you to be able to look at me the morning after we have spent the night together and not regret it. But maybe even that is wishing for the impossible, let alone dreaming about anything else.'

He walked away and Katherine heard the sound of the door slamming. She didn't move; she didn't think she could move. She closed her eyes, trying not to recall that pain in Jordan's voice, trying not to feel the empty throbbing of her body, trying not to wonder what he had meant.

What did Jordan *really* want from her?

CHAPTER TEN

THERE was no word from Jordan the next day. Katherine found herself staring into space, simply waiting for the phone to ring. Twice she picked it up to call his office but each time she changed her mind. What could she say to him after all? How could she explain how confused she felt? It was as though every single boundary around their relationship had disappeared, and she had no idea how she was supposed to act. She had no idea at all what Jordan really wanted from her!

When the doorbell rang just after lunch on the second day, she felt her heart lift painfully. The memory of what had happened in her bedroom was still so raw that even talking to Jordan was going to be difficult, but she wanted to see him so much!

It was such an anticlimax to open the door and find Peter outside that she couldn't speak at first. It was her brother who finally broke the silence, sounding a little unsure and quite unlike himself.

'Hello, Katherine. Can I come in?'

'Of course. I'm sorry, it's just that I wasn't expecting you...' She blinked, realising in a rush why she shouldn't have expected to see him. 'I thought you were still on your honeymoon! What's happened?'

'Guess!' Peter tried to smile as he walked into the sitting-room. 'Diane found out about the money. I...I think it's all over between us. We flew back this morning and she went home to her parents.'

'Oh, Peter!' Katherine sank down onto the sofa. 'How did she find out, though?'

'Because I told her.' He must have seen Katherine's surprise because he sighed. 'It seemed to me that starting married life with that kind of a secret was asking for trouble. I love Diane so much. I don't want to lie to her about anything!'

Katherine avoided his eyes. Peter wasn't alluding to *her* marriage but it could apply just the same. No marriage should be founded on anything other than total honesty, otherwise it didn't stand a chance of surviving.

'So what happens now?' she asked quietly. 'What are you going to do?'

'Find some way out of this mess. And get Diane back!' Peter laughed harshly. 'It's about time I started acting like an adult and sorted my life out. I have finally realised that.'

'Yes, I suppose you're right. Jordan went to see your creditors, and they agreed to give you a few weeks' breathing space. He also discovered exactly how much you owe.'

'I didn't want to worry you, Katherine—' Peter broke off and grimaced. 'That isn't quite true. I didn't want to think about how much trouble I was in. But it won't simply go away if I ignore it, will it? The money has to be repaid some way.'

'Jordan… Well, he might be prepared to lend you what you need.' Katherine looked down at her hands. She could feel her heart racing. She could save Peter from any more hurt—she alone could give him the chance to make his marriage work. She didn't dare think about what it would mean for her…

'I don't want him to!' Peter must have heard her gasp because he rushed to explain. 'Oh, I'm grateful for the offer, really I am, but I got into this mess and I shall get out of it. That's what I came to tell you—that I don't want Jordan sorting this out for me. I'm going to handle it myself and, after I have, then I shall be able to go to Diane and tell her that. Maybe she'll be prepared to talk then, and see what we can work out.'

'Are you sure, Peter? It's such a lot of money. Can you repay it?'

'No, I'm not sure I can do it, but I have to try.' Peter bent down to kiss her cheek. 'Thanks, Katherine. You've been the best sister in the world. I only wish I'd been a better brother. But, still, you've got Jordan. If I could be half the man he is then I'd be happy, believe me. Trouble is, there aren't many who measure up to him, are there? I know you two have had your problems, but take my advice and sort them out. What you and he could have is too good to risk losing!'

Katherine couldn't find anything to say. She saw Peter to the door, then went back inside. She wrapped her arms around herself, feeling the way her body shook in an agony of pain. What she and Jordan had was a sham, a travesty of what everyone believed their marriage to be! They had been fools to imagine it could have worked out any differently in the circumstances...

But things could change.

The thought slid into her mind, clear and uncluttered after all the confusion which had been there for days now. The situation had changed and could change even more if they both wanted it to. Jordan had told her what he wanted, but what did *she* want? A divorce?

Her mind shied away from that idea, finding it oddly painful. She couldn't imagine not seeing Jordan again, not being part of his life, if only on the fringes of it. So if she didn't want a divorce then did she want them to carry on the way they had been, living this shallow existence?

Her mind skittered away from that as well, which left only one option open to her: marriage. A real marriage that was. And children? Was that what she wanted?

Katherine looked round the empty flat and suddenly she knew that the answer couldn't be found here. She couldn't decide until, like Peter, she faced up to her problems. She was going to see her father, and after that she would decide where her future lay—if it was with Jordan…as his wife!

Brooklands lay serene and golden under a clear June sky. Katherine swung the car in through the gates and experienced the little rush of pleasure she always got when she came back home.

The mellow stone of the old house was washed with soft light as the day faded, the profusion of flowers in the surrounding beds making brilliant splashes of colour. The house was almost four hundred years old, and Katherine's family had lived here since it had been built. It would be nice to think of her children playing in the gardens as she had done…

Her breath caught as she drew the car to a jerky halt by the house, barely conscious of the car already parked there. Her father was at the door even before she managed to get out, his face alight with pleasure.

'Darling, you've made it after all! Oh, it's so good to have you both here together at last.' Adam Carstairs kissed his daughter's cheek, then linked his hand through her arm. 'Come in, come in! Leave Hodges to fetch your case.'

Katherine frowned as she let herself be led into the house. 'Both of us? Is Peter here as well?'

'Peter? Why, of course not! He's still on his honeymoon, isn't he?' Adam stopped and patted her arm. 'Still got your head in the clouds, I see. No, I meant Jordan has already arrived. He was just telling me that he wasn't sure if you would be able to make it, but here you are!'

Katherine felt her head swim. She glanced over her shoulder, suddenly realising that the big dark saloon parked in the drive was Jordan's car. She had never given any thought to the fact that he might be here!

Adam urged her into the small sitting-room at the rear of the house. 'Go along in, darling. Mrs Hodges has just brought in the tea tray so you couldn't have timed your arrival better. I'll just go and sort out your luggage.'

Katherine started to protest but her father had already gone hurrying off. She pushed the door open, knowing who she would find even before she saw the man who was standing looking out of the window. Her pulse seemed to quicken as she looked at him, the blood making her body feel heavy and hot. She looked at Jordan as he stood there with his head bowed and his shoulders hunched, and she felt so many things which would have been unthinkable just a week ago.

A week ago she'd had her defences firmly shored up, and nothing had seemed capable of breaking through them. But Jordan had. He had slipped through the barriers on Peter's wedding day, had opened the gap a bit wider when he'd been ill that night, and had forged an even bigger hole when he had told her about his past, then made that confession about not having made love to any other woman since their marriage...

Little by little, Jordan had broken through her defences, but why? That was the question she wanted to hear the answer to most—the one which scared her most as well!

'So you decided to come after all, Katherine. I didn't think you would, which is why I made your apologies to Adam.'

He didn't even need to look round to know she was there, it seemed. Katherine felt a ripple spread through her body although she couldn't understand what caused it. She took a deep breath as she went and sat down by the table where the tea tray was set.

'That was thoughtful of you. To be honest I'd completely forgotten about Daddy's invitation. I only came here on a whim,' she said to cover her nervousness.

She picked up the teapot, steadying it when she heard the low oath Jordan bit out. She looked at him and felt her face flood with colour when she saw the anger in his eyes. 'Jordan, what...?'

'You never miss an opportunity, do you? You never overlook a chance to make sure that I know exactly where I come in the pecking order. Thank you, Katherine, I am perfectly aware that you successfully forget all about me without you needing to rub it in!'

Katherine was stunned. 'But I didn't mean...'

'I know what you meant! But don't worry, I shall make some excuse to Adam and get out of your way.'

He strode towards the door and Katherine suddenly realised that he intended leaving there and then. She shot to her feet, completely forgetting that she was still holding the pot. Hot tea shot from its spout and soaked through the skirt of her cotton dress, and she cried out in pain, dropping the teapot.

Jordan looked round and seemed to take in the situation at a glance. Before Katherine could even think what to do, he had swept her up into his arms and was racing up the stairs with her. He kicked open the door to one of the bathrooms and set her down in the shower stall, then turned on the water, twisting the dial to cold as he lifted her skirt and aimed the jet at her thigh.

Katherine winced as the icy water hit the angry red scald mark. 'That stings!'

'It will stop it blistering. Stand still.' Jordan glared up at her, his blue eyes still full of anger and a pain which hurt her even more than the hot tea had done. So tough on the outside, she thought, so determined and wilful in getting what he wanted, yet she could hurt him this much. It didn't seem right.

She rested her hand on his shoulder as though to steady herself, yet she knew that in her own way she was trying to apologise. Jordan's eyes held hers in a look which seemed to see right inside her mind, but she didn't try to avoid it.

Let him see how she felt, she thought with sudden recklessness. Heaven knew, it couldn't make things worse than they already were!

He gave a slow smile and, even as she saw it start to curl the corners of his mouth, Katherine felt his shoulder relax as the anger drained out of him. 'Three falls, two submissions or a knock-out, Katherine?'

'What?' Her fingers dug a little deeper into his shoulder as she steadied herself. The water was still beating down onto her bare thigh, running down her legs, soaking into her dress even though Jordan was holding it out of the direct path of the jet. It was icy cold, yet she could feel the heat burning under her skin and sending waves through her whole body. Ice-cold on the outside, so hot beneath...

She took a shaky breath, her eyes luminous as they locked with his. 'I...I don't understand...what you mean,' she whispered.

He let go of the nozzle, seemingly uncaring that water

shot across the bathroom and soaked through the thin cotton shirt he was wearing. His eyes were darkest blue as they held hers, like the depths of the ocean. She could drown in them, she thought hazily, sink right to the bottom and never come up again.

'It's how you determine the winner in a wrestling match—three falls, two submissions, or a straightforward knock-out.'

His voice was husky with amusement, but she knew deep down that it was merely a cover for everything else he felt. She reached out and switched off the water, and the silence was suddenly deafening.

'Is that what you want, Jordan? To be declared the winner? What are you going for? A fall, a knock-out, or…or…?' She faltered.

He bent and lifted her out of the bath, and he held her even though there was no need to do so—because Katherine wasn't about to go anywhere; both of them knew that. He bent and brushed her mouth with his, although he didn't attempt to kiss her.

'One submission will do, my sweet. Just one small submission will be more than enough…'

His breath was warm and sweet on her mouth, on her cheek, then on her temple as he rubbed his lips against her in the most sensual of caresses. Katherine felt her stomach coil and knot, felt the tension spiral lower and lower until it reached the very centre of her being. She closed her eyes on a sudden wave of longing so intense that it was painful.

'Is one enough? Are you sure it's all you want, Jordan?'

'It's enough to start with, more than enough to be going on with…' His mouth moved again, skimming down her cheek, and she jumped as she felt him bite the cord in her neck, although he didn't do it hard enough to hurt her. She gave a soft little whimper, aching to feel his mouth on her again there, to feel it on other parts of her.

Her hands came up to twine around his neck, her body moulding to the shape of his. Their clothes were wet, proving less a barrier than a seductive stimulation—the rasp of wet cotton as her breasts brushed against his chest, the way the fabric clung and outlined her hardening nipples, the thrust of his aroused body through her soaked skirt…

'Katherine? Are you all right, darling?'

Adam Carstairs' concerned voice broke the spell. Jordan gave a heavy groan as he leant his forehead against hers and closed his eyes. 'Who said families are a blessing?'

Katherine took her courage in both hands. Maybe she was being a fool, maybe she would regret it… For a second the fears swirled and thickened, then faded as she realised that there was only one way she would ever find out.

'Wait until we have a child running about. I'm no expert, but I imagine we'll soon realise what having a family really means.'

He went so still that she thought he must have stopped breathing. His hands bit into her flesh as he clasped her shoulders and set her from him so that he could look into her face. 'Does that mean what I think it does?'

She eased herself away from him, and whisked herself out of the bathroom door. 'Could do.' She gave a teasing little laugh, wondering wildly how she could feel like teasing him over something so important! 'Would you say that was one submission each, Jordan? Or a full knock-out?'

'Katherine…'

She heard him roar her name but she didn't stop. She hurried into the room she'd had since she was a child, and closed the door. She looked round at all the childhood treasures—the posters and toys, the remnants of her past life—and took a deep breath.

She was no longer a child. She wasn't simply someone's daughter. She was a woman now. And soon she really would be Jordan's wife!

'Well, I must say that it has been a very pleasant evening, even though both of you seem to have a lot on your minds.'

Adam Carstairs picked up his glass and finished the last of the small measure of wine he was allowed to have with his meals. He smiled as he glanced from Katherine to Jordan. 'I have a feeling that I'm *de trop*, as they say, so I shall bid you both goodnight.'

Katherine got to her feet as her father rose. 'Honestly, Daddy, there's no need!' She glanced at Jordan and blushed as she saw the way he was watching her.

All through the meal she had been aware of him doing just that. Oh, he had been as urbane as ever—making conversation with Adam, including her in it—but underneath it all, they had both known what they were thinking about, what was going to happen…soon.

Adam kissed her cheek, his lined face full of tenderness. 'Katherine, darling, I may be old but I haven't forgotten how it feels!' He looked at Jordan, and it seemed almost as though he was addressing his comments to the younger man. 'I'm so pleased for you. I had been half-afraid… Well, none of that matters now. Goodnight, both of you.'

He made his way slowly to the door and closed it

behind him. Katherine felt her throat lock on a spasm of nerves as she realised that she and Jordan were alone at last. Suddenly she wasn't sure that she could handle what must be inevitable after what she had said before.

Her hands clenched as all the old fears ate away at her. What if she was making a mistake? What if it turned out exactly as she had feared...?

'It isn't too late to change your mind, Katherine. I won't force you into something you don't want.'

Jordan's voice grated. He was staring down at his glass, although Katherine noticed that he hadn't drunk more than a sip of the wine. Had he been afraid that he wouldn't be able to control himself if he had drunk it?

She sensed that was so. Jordan would never take what she wasn't willing to give, never demand more than she felt able to offer him. Even on their wedding night he had held back until he had been sure it was what she'd wanted!

Katherine walked round the table to where he sat, and held out her hand. 'Shall we go up now?'

For a moment he sat absolutely still, before he slowly rose to his feet, big and powerful as he towered over her. He took her hand and lifted it to his lips, brushing her knuckles with a kiss of such tenderness that Katherine felt her eyes mist with tears.

'You won't regret this, Katherine? You won't wake in the morning and wish it hadn't happened?'

Even now he was giving her the chance to back out, even now, when she could almost taste the desire he felt for her.

She reached up and brushed his cheek with a kiss. 'No. I won't regret it, Jordan. I only hope that you won't either. I hope that I can give you what you want from me.'

He didn't answer as he led her from the room, but perhaps he couldn't do that. There were no certainties, no guarantees for either of them. This must be just as difficult for him as it was for her, and the realisation eased so much of her fear.

Jordan led her into the big, airy bedroom that her father had insisted they should have. The windows were open to let in the soft June night. A sliver of moon shone across the bed, making any other light unnecessary.

He drew her into his arms and just held her for a long while, his face against her hair, his hands resting lightly against her back. Katherine rested against him, surprised at how right it felt to have him hold her this way.

He drew back at last, his face shadowed as he turned, so that the light was behind him although it played directly on her. Katherine felt heat shimmer through her veins as she felt his hands move to the tiny buttons which fastened the bodice of her dress, so gentle as he began to work them free.

She held her breath, feeling his fingertips brush her heated skin as he opened each button in turn until the two edges of the dress parted. The day had been so hot that she hadn't been able to face the thought of wearing a bra, and all there was between her breasts and Jordan's hands were the two thin pieces of cloth...

She lifted her hands and slowly drew the dress off her shoulders, and let it fall in a soft whisper at her feet. Jordan didn't move as she stood there, her body bare apart from the tiny silk panties which were all she wore now. Katherine felt her heart drumming inside her, felt the wash of heat which swept over her. What was Jordan thinking as he stood there?

Her eyes rose to his face at last, and she saw the wild glitter in his eyes just a second before he bent and kissed her with a hunger that left no room for thought. His mouth was urgent, his lips cool on the outside and burning with passion underneath.

'Katherine…my love…'

His voice whispered in the silence as he raised his head and stared into her face, searching for—what? Some sign that she was afraid, that she was regretting what was happening? A low, throaty growl came from him as he obviously found no trace of either on the moonlit contours of her face.

'I've waited so long for this…so long!'

There was a note of raw exultation in the words, an arrogance about the way he swept her off her feet and carried her over to the bed. Yet when he bent to lay her down on it he did it so gently, so carefully. Katherine reached up and framed his face, marvelling that behind such physical strength there could be such gentleness, that behind such deep desire there could be tenderness.

He turned his face so that he could kiss each of her palms, then bent and pressed his lips to the base of her throat, where the pulse was beating so wildly. Katherine shivered as she felt his mouth against her skin, shivered again as she felt it slide lower…

Her breath exhaled in a tiny gasp, her hands falling to her sides, her fingers clenching as she felt his mouth close over her nipple, felt the warm, moist sweep of his tongue, the gentle rasp of his teeth.

'Jordan!'

His name seemed to come from some place deep inside her, raw and aching with her need, when she let it come from her lips. He raised his head, laughing gently as he saw her face, and the laughter turned to a groan of longing so suddenly that it both shocked and exhilarated her.

'God, Katherine, you have no idea what you do to me…!'

His mouth found her breasts again, his hands easing the silk panties down her hips so that she was completely naked. Katherine tugged at the buttons on his shirt, suddenly impatient to touch him, to feel his body next to hers without any barriers in the way. One of the buttons tore off in her haste and shot across the room, and she gasped in dismay, then laughed out loud. What did it matter about one little button? What did anything matter apart from this?

Jordan's shirt landed on the floor and the rest of his clothes followed it until she could feel him against her, every inch of his skin touching hers. She ran her hands down his back, feeling the muscles shiver and dance beneath her touch. So much strength in these muscles, yet she made him tremble; *she* was the one with that much power!

'Witch! You know damned well you drive me insane, and you enjoy it, don't you? Even on our wedding night you knew how much I wanted you, knew that I was like putty in your hands!'

Katherine smiled up at him, seeing the harshness in his eyes, as though he hated to make such a confession. Her hand slid round to his chest, moved lower over his flat stomach, lower still… 'Not putty, Jordan.'

He laughed deeply, burying his face in her throat. 'I don't give a damn what I am right now. Just cast your spell, Katherine. That is all I ask!' He raised his head and stared at her. 'And maybe we shall find that it's all we need.'

'Jordan…' She couldn't finish what she'd been going to say, couldn't ask him what he'd meant because he took her mouth again.

The kiss seemed to go on and on, spinning them away into a time and place where nothing mattered apart from the world of pleasure they were creating. And when at last Jordan joined with her in the ultimate act of giving between man and woman, Katherine knew that it was the one place she wanted to be—just her and Jordan…together.

Did she have any regrets?

Katherine searched her heart as she watched Jordan sleeping, but it was empty of anything other than a peace and contentment she couldn't recall feeling before. The hours she'd spent in his arms had been the most magical of her life so how could she regret them?

She slid from the bed as quietly as she could so as not to disturb him. It was only just dawn and she didn't want him waking up just yet…although the idea did hold a certain temptation!

Her heart leapt with sweet anticipation as she half turned, wondering if she should climb back into the bed and wake him…

But maybe that was how passion claimed its victims—by making them long for more and more, by turning desire into something uncontrollable and voracious, something ugly and despicable.

She went cold as the thought slid into her mind. For a moment fear rose inside her as the old demons rushed back to taunt her before she took a deep breath. What she and Jordan had shared last night hadn't been ugly or despicable! It had been clean and pure and beautiful.

The demons slunk back into the dark recesses of her mind, but suddenly Katherine knew that she had to rid herself of them once and for all. She couldn't live like this—haunted by them, afraid to really live at all. She wasn't her mother! She didn't need a dozen men to satisfy her appetites but one man, this man, the man who was her husband! She loved Jordan, and…

She grasped the windowsill and held onto it as the room began to spin. She loved Jordan? How? Why? When?

Questions ran thick and fast through her head, the answers eluding her. She had no idea how or why, she simply did. She loved Jordan and that was why she had given herself to him so totally; that was why he had such power to disturb her when other men had left her unmoved! It was all so simple that she marvelled she hadn't understood it before, but it would take some getting used to!

She dressed quickly, anxious now that Jordan shouldn't wake. She needed time to herself, to allow the realisation to settle into her mind, before she decided what she must do about it.

Her hands shook as she buttoned her dress and recalled how Jordan had unbuttoned it… She blanked out the thought because it simply confused things.

Katherine let herself out of the house and took the path leading to the lake. The morning air was cool, but she didn't feel its chill. She was so lost in a world of her own that she didn't even notice the figure sitting in the shadows of the old summer-house until her father spoke.

'You're up early, darling. Couldn't you sleep?'

'Daddy!' She pressed a hand to her heart and smiled. 'You gave me a fright.' She glanced at him in sudden concern as she realised that he was dressed and shaved. 'But never mind about me being up, what are you doing here so early?'

'Oh, you don't need much sleep when you get to my

age, Katherine. In fact, it seems rather a shame to waste what time you have left by sleeping it away.'

Katherine joined in his gentle laughter, although it grieved her to think that one day her father might not be around. He had been her mainstay throughout all the bad times.

'I had a letter from your mother last week, Katherine. She sends you her love.'

Had Adam somehow latched onto her thoughts? Maybe. But Katherine wished he hadn't spoken about her mother, especially not now. She plucked a blade of long grass and ran it between her fingers as she avoided his eyes. 'Does she?'

'Your mother loves you, darling,' Adam said gently. 'Don't you know that?'

Katherine tossed the grass away. She could feel the pain rising inside her as bitter as bile. 'I don't think that Mother has any idea what love is, quite frankly! If she loved either Peter or me then why did she leave? Why did she decide that chasing one man after another was far more important than we were? The only thing Mother cared for was her own pleasure, her own disgusting appetites!'

Her father turned pale. 'Katherine, that simply isn't true!'

'No? Are you trying to deny that Mother had one affair after another?'

'You don't understand. Really, darling, you have it all wrong.' Adam sounded distraught, and Katherine came to her senses all of a sudden. What was she doing, upsetting him like this?

'I'm sorry, Daddy. I shouldn't have said that. Please try to forget it.'

He shook his head. 'No. I've let this ride for too long.

I should never have allowed your mother to persuade me
not to tell you the truth. It was wrong, and it's about
time you knew what really went on, Katherine.'

He took a deep breath, as though steeling himself for
what he had to say. 'Yes, your mother had affairs—
although not as many as the gossip would have folk
believe. But I drove her to them. It was my fault,
Katherine.'

'Yours? I don't understand.' Katherine could hear the
bewilderment in her voice. When Adam drew her down
to sit beside him she didn't demur.

'I married your mother not because I was in love with
her but because she came from a wealthy family. I won't
go into the details; suffice it to say that at the time the
fortunes of the Carstairs were very shaky. I'm not proud
to admit what I did—even less proud of the fact that
Caroline had no idea. She thought I loved her, you see,
because she loved me very deeply.'

'Daddy...I had no idea!'

'Why should you?' Adam's expression was pained.
'You were little more than a child when it all blew up
in our faces, Peter even younger. You were too young
to appreciate what was behind all the arguments.' He
sighed sadly. 'You see, I met the woman I had been in
love with before I married your mother. I had broken
off the relationship when I realised what had to be done
to save the family and I hadn't seen her since. Then,
quite by chance, we met again.'

He sighed again, as though he had thought about this
many times. Katherine covered his hand with her own,
wanting to comfort him, and he smiled sadly at her.

'We had an affair. Maybe it was inevitable—maybe
that is just an excuse. But it happened, and your mother
found out. We said a lot of harsh things to one another,

but the most inexcusable thing was that I told Caroline the truth about why I had married her.' His voice broke. 'I...I think it broke her heart.'

Katherine felt her eyes fill with tears. How must her mother have felt, hearing that? It must have been dreadful for her.

Adam continued in a weary tone. 'After that, Caroline changed. It was as though she had to prove to herself and to me that although I hadn't wanted her other men could. I don't think she got any pleasure from the affairs she had, which is the most tragic thing of all. It simply wasn't in her nature to act the way she did. In the end, the situation became unbearable for everyone. We agreed that it was better we parted, and Caroline left.

'She could easily have taken you and Peter with her, but she cared too much to uproot you from everything you knew. She wanted you both to have security and stability, and she couldn't offer you those when she had no idea where she would be living.'

'I had no idea,' Katherine confessed softly.

'I know you didn't.' Adam looked straight into her eyes. 'Your mother refused to let me explain the situation to you because she didn't want you thinking badly of me, darling. She said that you didn't need all your illusions shattered, and that to rob you of your belief in me would do untold damage. You were fifteen at the time and she knew the rumours you'd heard; she didn't want you being hurt any more than you had been already.'

Adam stood up abruptly, as though he couldn't bear to say anything more. 'I only hope we didn't make a mistake about that. I know all those stories you heard about your mother must have left their mark, even though you've never spoken about it until now. Still, seeing you and Jordan together last night makes me hope not—although I've had my doubts this past year.'

'I love him, Daddy.' Katherine whispered brokenly. It was hard to take in what she had heard, yet she knew it was the truth. Her heart ached at what her mother had gone through, the way she must have suffered. She could understand the agony Caroline must have felt on discovering that the man she loved had used her, could understand too why her mother had felt driven to do what she had.

It hadn't been passion which had driven Caroline into those other men's arms but a desperate attempt to prove to herself that she was worth loving. It was so tragic.

Adam smiled. 'That's all I need to hear. It means you can't go wrong, as I did, my darling.'

Katherine closed her eyes as her father returned to the house, trying to absorb everything she had learned. It wasn't easy, yet it felt as though suddenly a huge burden had been lifted from her shoulders and she'd been set free—free to be herself, not Caroline's daughter, free to love Jordan and feel that desire for him without fear, free to look towards the future…

'Katherine?'

She opened her eyes as Jordan came to stand beside the bench and smiled up at him, feeling the warm wash of joy and relief filling her heart. 'I thought you were asleep.'

His smile was reflective. 'Mmm, I was until I realised you'd gone missing. Not running out on me, sweetheart, I hope?'

His tone was light enough, but his eyes hinted that there was more to the simple question. Katherine stood up and slid her hand through his arm. 'Not a chance of that, Mr James. We've still got the knock-out to go for!'

He bent and kissed her quickly, but there was hunger beneath the kiss, desire turning it into an assault on her senses. Katherine gasped as he let her go, but she didn't try to hide how she felt.

'No regrets, Katherine?'

She looked straight into his eyes, wanting him to believe her. 'No regrets at all, Jordan. How about you?'

He shook his head. 'No. I...' He stopped, as though not quite sure whether to continue, then glanced over his shoulder. 'I suppose we'd better get back. Adam said something about breakfast, and I for one am starving, Mrs James.'

Katherine grinned, loving to hear him call her that. 'Must have been the exercise last night. Come along, then. I'd hate you to fade away before my eyes.'

Jordan took her hand and kissed it quickly. 'I hope that means you have plans for me?'

She laughed, feeling her senses stir at the light caress. 'Could do. You'll just have to wait and see, won't you?' She pulled her hand free and shot off. 'Race you back for starters!'

Jordan laughed out loud. He was hard on her heels all the way up the path. Katherine knew that he could easily have beaten her, but he let her win.

Her father was just coming out of his study as they both flew through the door, and he beamed at them.

'You two look as though you're having fun.' His face sobered. 'More than poor Peter. That boy does get himself into some scrapes, doesn't he? That was him on the phone just now, to say that he's coming to stay for a few days. You should have told me he was back from his honeymoon, darling. I expect you didn't want to worry me, though.'

'When did he get back?' Jordan's voice grated

harshly. He removed his arm from Katherine's shoulders where he had looped it so casually just moments before. She shot him a quick look, and shivered as she saw the coldness which had settled over his face.

'I'm not sure. He popped round to see you, didn't he, Katherine? When was that?'

'Just after lunch yesterday.' Her voice sounded thin and shallow. Why? Because she felt suddenly afraid?

'Just before you set off down here, was that, Katherine? Before you had that sudden urge to visit your father. Quite forgetting that I would be here, of course.'

Katherine licked her lips, but she couldn't seem to ease their dryness. The way Jordan was looking at her chilled her to her soul. 'I had forgotten about Daddy's invitation. I explained that to you.'

'Of course you did! Sorry, sweetheart. How on earth could I have forgotten that?' Jordan smiled, but if anything his expression was grimmer. He turned to Adam, who was watching the exchange with obvious bewilderment. 'Did Peter have anything else to say, as a matter of interest?'

'I… Er…oh, yes, just that he was very grateful for your offer to help him.' Adam smiled at Katherine, obviously seeking to ease the tension which was evident to them all. 'Thank heavens we have Jordan around to sort out our problems!'

'But what are families for? Isn't that right, Katherine? I mean, how could I refuse to help my wife's family when I have such an incentive to do so now?'

'Jordan, you…'

He didn't appear to hear her and he addressed Adam. 'I hope it doesn't make a mess of your plans, but I'm afraid I shall have to return to London.'

'Oh, what a shame. I had hoped that you would both be able to stay the weekend.'

Adam sounded confused by the sudden change of plans, but Katherine understood. Jordan believed that she had slept with him so that he would help Peter, that the reason she wanted to make their marriage a real one in every sense was because she had decided to accept his terms!

'Jordan, please, you don't—'

'Of course, you must stay, Katherine.' He cut her off, and his eyes were glacial behind the smiling mask as he looked at her. 'You stay and make sure that your brother knows he has nothing more to worry about.'

CHAPTER ELEVEN

'JORDAN, we have to talk.'

Jordan was packing clothes into an overnight bag when Katherine went into the bedroom. He didn't look round, simply carried on with what he was doing. He turned to go to the wardrobe, then stopped when she failed to move out of his way.

'Excuse me.'

Katherine shivered as she heard the icy note in his voice, such a contrast to how he had spoken to her earlier. 'Did you hear me, Jordan? We have to talk! You've got this all wrong.'

'I don't think so.' He stepped around her to take a pair of trousers off a hanger. He put them in the bag, then zipped up the top before heading for the door.

'Wait! You can't just walk off like this!'

'Why not? What else needs to be said? I think everything is sorted out at last, isn't it, Katherine? Oh, apart from one very important detail, of course.'

A bitter smile twisted his beautiful mouth as he strode to the small desk by the window—the same mouth which had kissed her, caressed her, drawn an unbridled response from her just hours before...

'What?' Katherine suddenly realised what he had said. She watched in confusion as he wrote in sure, swift strokes, then he tossed the pen onto the desk and came over to her.

'I nearly forgot this. How remiss of me. I'm glad you reminded me, Katherine. After all, you earned it.' His eyes were like shards of ice as they travelled the length of her body and came back to her face in a look which was nothing less than an insult. 'Yes, you most definitely earned it.'

Katherine took the paper he'd thrust into her hand, feeling sick and shaken at the way he had looked at her so that it was a moment before she realised what it was. Her eyes flew to his as her face turned starkly white.

'How could you, Jordan? How could you?'

He flicked the cheque with his finger and smiled thinly. 'I thought you'd be pleased, Katherine. It's a lot of money. But then it can't have been easy playing the sacrificial lamb, although you did it so well that you had me fooled. I actually thought that you had decided to try to make a go of our marriage because you wanted to. How very arrogant of me, eh?

'You simply couldn't bring yourself to tell me that after having spoken to Peter you finally made up your mind where your duty lay. Still, I doubt I've ever enjoyed spending a hundred grand quite as much, so that's some compensation.'

The sound of her hand striking his cheek seemed even louder in the silence than it should have done. Katherine went even whiter, if that was possible. She stared in horror at the reddening mark on his face, unable to believe she had actually hit him.

Jordan's hands clenched before he swung round. Katherine felt tears spill from her eyes and run down her face. 'I'm sorry, Jordan. I...I didn't mean to do that.'

He didn't bother to look at her as he opened the door. 'Don't worry about it. I shan't.'

'Don't go. Please, Jordan, don't leave like this. You've got this all wrong. You have to let me explain...'

'No!' He swung round at that, fury glittering in his

eyes, the mark of her hand staining his cheek. 'I don't have to listen to anything you say, not one lie or excuse. I know why you came down here yesterday and I know why you slept with me last night. What else is there to add? Apart from the fact that I've suddenly come to my senses and realised what a fool I've been.'

He gave her a look of bitter contempt. 'I thought that I'd be happy if you agreed to my terms, but I suddenly find that the idea sticks in my throat. It's a salutary lesson to discover that getting what you want doesn't always work out how you imagined it would.'

'Jordan, please! Why won't you listen to me?'

'Because there is no point. One thing I have learned over the years is that sometimes it's better simply to cut your losses and move on. Maybe last night achieved something after all—something apart from you earning the money to pay your brother's debts, of course. Maybe it helped get you out of my system, and that can't be a bad thing!'

He strode out of the door without giving her the chance to say anything more. Katherine listened to his footsteps going down the stairs and away from her.

'Jordan…Jordan.' She whispered his name but he didn't hear her. It wouldn't have made any difference if he had. Jordan was walking out of her life, and he was never coming back.

June drifted past, taking with it the warm weather. July brought only rain. Katherine awoke each day to grey skies. They matched the way she felt—grey and colourless, as though the life had gone out of her.

She'd not heard a word from Jordan and had no idea even whether he was in the country or not. Each day she woke wondering if today would be the day that he contacted her, but it never happened.

She spoke to both her father and Peter on the telephone regularly and knew that they were worried about her, even though she'd refused to discuss the situation with either of them. She couldn't bear to talk about what had happened with anyone.

Peter had come to some arrangement with his creditors and was starting to pay them back. He had taken on a second job on the weekends, and, with the money from that and the fact that he had sold his car and cut his spending to the bone, he was starting to make some headway.

Katherine admired his determination, although there was a certain irony in the fact that he hadn't needed her help in the end. If only... But what was the point in wishing for the impossible?

It was the middle of July when she couldn't stand the waiting any longer and plucked up the courage to ring Jordan's office, using the excuse that she needed to speak to him but had lost his phone number. She wasn't sure who was the more embarrassed when his secretary carefully explained that he was in London, staying at his club.

Katherine felt as though she had hit rock-bottom then. She wasn't even able to make the excuse that he was in some far-flung corner of the globe. He was here in the city and could have contacted her if he had wanted to.

She made dinner that evening and forced herself to eat a little of it before throwing the rest away. Her appetite was non-existent and she had lost a great deal of weight. When she heard the doorbell ringing it never even crossed her mind that it might be Jordan. There was no point in hoping for that now.

Charles was standing outside, looking faintly nervous, as though he wasn't sure of his welcome. 'Hello, Katherine. I...I thought I would just call round to see how you are.'

'Charles.' Her tone lacked any warmth, because after their last encounter she wasn't sure she wanted to speak to him.

'Can I come in for a moment?' He gave the door a little push and stepped inside the hallway. Katherine could either invite him in or ask him to leave, and the latter, with all the unpleasantness it might cause, seemed beyond her.

She led the way into the sitting-room, making sure that he realised how unhappy she was about what he had done.

'Sorry.' He gave her a conciliatory smile. 'That was a bit presumptuous of me. It's just that I could tell how reluctant you were to invite me in. Not that I can blame you. I made a complete idiot of myself, didn't I?'

He sounded so remorseful that Katherine softened. 'You did. I don't know what came over you, Charles.' She glanced down. 'I...I'm sorry that you misunderstood and that you lost your job because of it.'

Charles shrugged. 'I can't say that I've shed too many tears over that. Jordan made sure I was handsomely paid off, and to tell the truth I did find the job a bit much at times.'

He looked round, then took a deep breath. 'I keep in touch with a few people at the office, though, so I hear what's going on.'

'Do you?' Katherine picked up the sherry decanter. 'Would you like a drink?'

'Yes. Lovely. Thank you.' He sounded a lot more comfortable all of a sudden, as though her offer had settled his mind. Katherine wasn't sure if it had been wise, but there was little she could do now. She poured them both a small sherry and handed him a glass. She jumped as he took it from her and caught hold of her hand.

'I've heard all about you and Jordan, Katherine.'

'I've no idea what you mean.' Katherine tried to move away, but Charles still held onto her.

'Of course you have! God damn it, Katherine, what kind of a marriage is it if you don't even know where your own husband is? What kind of a marriage is it if he doesn't bother to tell you where he's staying?'

The words were so bitterly poignant that Katherine's throat closed, and Charles evidently took her silence as an encouraging sign. He came to his feet and took hold of her by the shoulders.

'I was a fool to take you by surprise as I did that day in the office, but now you've had time to think about what I said and you know I'm right. Jordan doesn't love you like I do. He doesn't deserve you! He's nothing but a self-centred bastard who enjoys playing God with other people's lives! Leave him, Katherine, and come away with me.'

'How dare you?' Katherine's temper roared to life. After the weeks of lethargy it shocked her whole system. Her eyes blazed as she pushed Charles away. 'How dare you say that about my husband? Who do you think you are, coming here and calling him names? Jordan is twice the man you'll ever be, Charles. He is honest and trust-worthy, and when he makes a promise he sticks to it…to the letter. So don't you dare come into my home and call the man I love a bastard or any other such name. Get out!'

'Katherine! I…'

'No! I won't listen to another word. Please leave, Charles. And do not come back!'

Katherine stood where she was as Charles made his way to the door. He looked back and seemed about to say something before he obviously changed his mind. Katherine heard the door slam, and bit back a bitter little laugh.

She was getting rather good at this, at watching people leaving and listening to doors closing. Was this what her life was going to entail from now on? Being left behind, being left waiting?

Her temper moved another notch up the scale until the blood raced through her veins. It felt wonderful, marvellous. She felt alive and in control, and suddenly she knew that she was no longer prepared to step aside while others decided her fate. She was her own woman and she would shape her own future!

She stormed into the bedroom and found her raincoat. She dragged it on, then stopped as she caught sight of herself in the mirror. Her heart skipped a beat. She was also Jordan's wife…and it was about time he remembered that!

The taxi dropped her off right in front of the imposing building. Katherine paid the fare, but she was conscious of the driver's eyes following her as she mounted the steps. She had a good idea what he was thinking as he watched her pushing open the glass doors.

There was a steward on duty behind an old-fashioned desk. He looked up and did a doubletake as he saw her, a woman, daring to enter this last bastion of male supremacy.

'I… Ahem. Can I help you, madam?'

Katherine smiled thinly as she looked round. Heavy

oak panelling, a lot of fusty pictures of past members—
it was definitely not to her taste. She was rather surprised
that it should be Jordan's taste either, but still…

'Madam? I'm afraid this is a gentlemen's club.
Perhaps you have the wrong address? I could call you a
cab?'

Katherine shook her head. 'I have the right address. I
wish to see my husband, Jordan James. Please inform
him that I am here.'

The steward looked decidedly uncomfortable, and
Katherine hid a grim little smile. She would bet a pound
to a penny he was worrying about something untoward
happening, like an unsavoury marital tiff. Heaven forbid!

'I'm not sure if Mr James is available at present.' The
man cleared his throat. 'In fact, I don't think he has
returned yet. Perhaps I can pass on a message for you,
madam?'

'That won't be necessary. I shall wait.'

Katherine headed for the stairs, following the sign
marked 'library'. She swept up them, passing an elderly
gentleman just coming down who looked as though he
was about to have a heart attack as he spotted a female
of the species within the hallowed halls.

'Really, madam, I must protest! Ladies are not allowed inside the club. It's one of our strictest rules!'

The steward snapped around her heels like a pesky
terrier. Katherine stopped and drew herself up. She
wasn't her father's daughter for nothing, descended from
generations of British aristocracy. 'Then it is way past
time the rules were changed. Now, may I suggest that
you go and see if my husband has returned? That way
we won't need to ruffle the feathers of any more members, will we?'

She didn't bother waiting for the man to reply as she

carried on up the stairs, following the signs until she arrived at the library. She opened the door and wrinkled her nose at the musty smell of mildew on leather. There was nobody in the room—not that it would have bothered her if there had been. She had come to see Jordan, and see him she would!

She tossed her raincoat onto one of the high-backed leather chairs then started to pace the worn carpet. Now that she was thinking clearly for the first time in weeks she was furious. How dared Jordan treat her the way he had? How dared he say all those dreadful things to her? How dared he *accuse* her then not allow her to explain…?

'What the hell are you doing here?'

The door opened and Jordan was suddenly in the room. Katherine came to an abrupt halt, her hair swirling around her shoulders. Her face was starkly white so that her eyes seemed almost black, glittering with the anger she felt. For a moment the sight of him made her senses swirl dangerously, and then he closed the door with an angry snap and everything shot sharply back into focus: him, her, why she had come!

'I asked you what you mean by coming here. If I had wanted to speak to you, Katherine, then I would have got in touch. Now, I think it would be better if you left right away.'

He was standing with his back to the door and his legs astride, big and arrogant as he stood there and tried to dictate her life. Katherine felt her temper surge to almost dizzying heights, so that the momentary weakness melted before its heat.

'Do you?' She gave him a wide smile. 'Well, I'm afraid I've had it up to here with hearing what people think.' Her hand hovered at the level of her waist. She smiled at Jordan again. 'In fact I've had it to here—' her hand rose to her chest '—with being told what *I* should do. And I've had it right up to *here* listening to what *you* want!' Her hand came level with the top of her head before she let it drop abruptly. 'It's about time that I told you what I think, what I intend to do and what *I* want!'

Jordan's eyes glittered with fury as he took a step towards her. 'I'm not interested, Katherine. Understand? I don't give a damn any longer! Now, leave—before…'

She gave a low laugh, deliberately taunting him. She knew that it was playing with fire to incite his anger, but there was a seductive thrill to the idea of what might happen if she managed to make him lose control.

'Before…what? Before you make me leave? How? I remember very clearly you telling me that you would never lift a finger to me. But then how can I believe that you're a man of your word when you have shown me how much that is worth in the past few weeks?'

'Why, you…' His hands bit into the tops of her arms, bruising her flesh, hurting her so that despite her determination she winced. Jordan stilled at once, and his blue eyes darkened with pain, as though…as though hurting her had hurt him more, Katherine thought shakily. And in a sudden flash everything fell into place, and she understood why he had set out to make their marriage real, what it was he really wanted from her.

Jordan loved her.

The realisation stunned her. She could feel it beating inside her with a rhythm which made her tremble with joy, yet he seemed to interpret that entirely the wrong way.

He pushed her away and turned to stride to the door, his voice hoarse with anguish. 'I want you to leave,

Katherine. I...I apologise for my roughness. I never meant to hurt you.'

She took a slow breath and let it out in the softest whisper, yet she saw him tense as though he had heard it. Maybe he had. Jordan was so attuned to her responses in some ways, and yet so deaf, dumb and blind to them in others. Maybe it was because he was afraid to believe what his heart was telling him. Love made fools out of even the cleverest people!

'I won't leave until I say what I came here to say. You can either stand there and listen or I shall make the sort of scene this place hasn't seen in years.' She shrugged when he looked round. 'Frankly, I don't care. People can come and take pictures if they like, but it won't stop me. I'm sick and tired of living a lie.'

He turned slowly. He was so tense that he moved like an automaton. Katherine guessed that he was afraid to show any sign of softening, afraid even to feel it. Jordan was fighting for his dignity, his pride, for everything which made him what he was, and she wouldn't take any of that away from him. She would never make him beg for what he wanted when she was so willing to give it!

Her voice was cool and clear but her eyes blazed. 'I came to tell you that I love you, Jordan. I realised it that morning at Brooklands, but I doubt I fell in love with you that night.'

She laughed softly, watching his face, but he didn't move a muscle. She understood. 'I think I was probably in love with you long before then but fighting desperately not to face it. I didn't sleep with you so that you would give Peter the money. He'd already told me that he didn't want your help.'

She opened her bag, took out the cheque and tossed

it down on a nearby table. Jordan's eyes flickered to it, then returned to her face. Katherine wasn't certain, but there seemed to be a hint of warmth in them.

She took a slow step towards him, then another for good luck, even if it might not be good judgement. She was working by instinct now, nothing else; after all, this was the first time she had ever told a man that she loved him.

'I can't make you believe me. I can't prove that what I'm saying is true. I can only hope that you accept it. I love you, Jordan James. Without you my life has been as miserable as sin, and I fervently hope yours has been just as miserable these past few weeks. The solution is easy, but it's up to you now whether you take it.'

She took the last few steps, and paused, her brows arching slightly. 'Excuse me.'

He didn't move a muscle, although the expressions which chased across his face made Katherine feel giddy. She felt her heart pounding, and silently prayed that he would make the right decision for both of them...

He stepped aside and Katherine felt her heart break. She was blinded by tears as she reached for the handle. This was the end. She had tried and failed...

'Would you say that was two submissions each?'

Jordan's voice grated. Katherine felt every nerve in her body prickle to life. 'I...I don't think you can count properly. It's two to me, but only one to you, Jordan.'

'Then hadn't we better rectify that?' He spun her round so fast she gasped. His eyes blazed down at her, yet the smile he gave her was full of tenderness. 'I love you, Katherine. You are my heart, my soul, my life. I loved you long before we married and I shall love you until the day I die. Is that enough?'

'Yes...yes!' Joy shone in her eyes as she stared into

his face and saw the answer she had wanted written
there, the solution to everything. She went on tiptoe to
press her mouth to his, and felt the anguished shudder
which ran through him as he pulled her even closer and
held her as though he would never let her go. His mouth
was hungry for hers, his need for her so blatant that it
scented the very air around them, with passion swirling
in heavy, musky waves.

'I love you so much, Jordan!' Her voice was a whisper
when she had wanted it to be a shout, but he laughed in
exultation anyway.

'I know! It's what I've dreamed of for so long and
thought would never happen! Oh, Katherine, what fools
we've been to waste so much time.'

She touched his mouth with her fingers and felt them
tremble. She smiled up at him, her eyes telling him so
clearly how she felt that she heard him gasp. 'But think
what fun we're going to have making up for it, Jordan.'

'God!' He groaned deeply as he pulled her back into
his arms, then looked round in disbelief as there was a
loud knock at the door. 'Not again! I don't believe it!'

Katherine giggled at the expression on his face as he
let her go and went to answer the door. She picked up
her raincoat, then stopped as she saw the cheque still
lying on the table. She picked it up and tore it into
pieces, then watched them flutter to the floor like confetti
as Jordan came back. He glanced at the bits of paper
and for a moment there was a searing pain in his eyes.

Katherine shook her head. 'Don't! It doesn't matter,
not now.' She smiled at him, knowing in her heart that
it was true. 'So, who was that at the door? The steward
by any chance?'

He touched her cheek lightly, accepting what she said
even though she knew that it would take him a long time

to rid himself of guilt because of what he had done. 'Yes. The poor fellow was almost beside himself. Evidently Rule 26 in the members' handbook states, and I quote, ''Ladies may not be entertained within club premises except on stated days in the year.'''

Katherine's brows rose. 'And only when there's an ''r'' in the month, I presume?' She slid her hand into his. 'Well, it's not a problem. We shall just go somewhere else.' She gave Jordan a wicked smile. 'This is hardly the place for what I have in mind, nor, hopefully, for what you might have in mind. I don't think we're going to get very far without your co-operation, Jordan.'

He pulled her to him and held her close, then laughed as he saw her face colour. 'I think my co-operation is guaranteed, Katherine, wouldn't you agree?'

Katherine went outside and waited sedately while Jordan had a conciliatory word with the steward before they left. Not that it mattered. She wouldn't be coming back and neither would Jordan very often—and definitely not to stay!

The light from the street lamps filtered into the room and played across Jordan's bare chest. Katherine smoothed her hand over his skin, watching the light dapple her fingers. The bedroom was very quiet, the soft sound of their breathing all that broke the silence after the heady frenzy of their passion.

'Happy, Katherine?' Jordan tilted her face up and kissed her gently. His eyes were dark with love as they held hers. Katherine lifted her hand to his face and pressed it against his cheek.

'Happier than I thought it possible to be darling. I love you so much.'

'That's what I like to hear. I want nothing less than total adoration for the next…oh, sixty years at least.'

He settled her head into the hollow of his shoulder, his deep voice holding a wealth of tender amusement. Katherine smiled as she heard it. She turned her head and skimmed her lips up the side of his neck, and felt the shivering tingle of response which ran through him.

'Only sixty years, Jordan? Doesn't sound all that long to me. I don't know if I like the idea that you might tire of me so quickly.'

He laughed deeply as he let his hand slide down beneath the sheet and come to rest on the curve of her bare hip, and it was Katherine's turn to tremble. It didn't seem to matter that they had just made love with wild abandonment and reached a height of fulfilment she could never have dreamt of. She still wanted him even now, but it didn't scare her as it would have done once. Her passion for Jordan was as pure and natural as breathing, and just as vital. Maybe she should explain that to him, explain why she had been so afraid to face up to it before.

She tilted her head so that she could look into his face. 'I…I never realised how it could be, Jordan. I was always so afraid…'

Her voice tailed off, but he bent and kissed her. 'Tell me, Katherine. Let's not have any secrets. Tonight we start all over again, so let's start with a clean slate and then we need write only good things on it from here on.'

'Yes, you're right.' She relaxed against him, letting her hand drift softly back and forth across his chest. 'There have been so many secrets, haven't there? But I suppose the one which caused the most damage was my secret fear that I might turn out to be like my mother— or like I always imagined her to be.'

He stroked her hair tenderly. 'I know a little of what happened, darling.' He must have felt the start she gave because his hand stilled. 'That day, after the picnic, I went to see your father. I wanted to understand what you'd meant, you see. Oh, Adam only told me the bare bones of what had gone on, but I filled in the rest.' He lifted her face and looked at her. 'You were afraid of letting yourself feel desire for me in case you were unable to control your feelings. You were afraid that you might end up having affair after affair like your mother did. Am I right?'

Her eyes misted with tears. 'I never thought you'd guess, but it's true. That's why I was so…so afraid of letting myself respond to you.'

'Maybe I wouldn't have guessed if I hadn't needed to understand so desperately. I knew how you felt about me and I knew how afraid you were about *what* you felt. It didn't make sense until Adam told me the story and I put two and two together.' His voice broke. 'I was so scared, Katherine. Terrified that I might never get through to you because your fears were too deeply embedded!'

'Jordan…don't!' She kissed him hard, needing to offer him comfort. 'Is that why you didn't stay that night after the picnic?'

'Yes. I'd come back to the flat to see if we could talk through what I had learned. However, when I discovered you were gone I went through agonies, wondering what had happened to you. I knew you were upset and I was afraid that I'd pushed you too hard. And then you came back and… Well, everything erupted. The only problem was that I was terrified of ruining everything. I knew what lay behind your reluctance to make love with me and I was afraid that you would hate me for taking advantage of your vulnerability afterwards.'

'Reluctance?' Katherine laughed wryly. 'It would have been easier if I *had* been reluctant! I might have been able to cut you out of my life, but it proved impossible to do that after you came back for Peter's wedding.' She paused. 'It was impossible before that, too.'

'You mean what happened on our wedding night?'

'Yes. I hadn't expected that. I thought I had everything clear in my head. It was a business arrangement, nothing more. The trouble was you seemed to have such a strange effect on me whenever I saw you. I tried to pretend it wasn't happening and closed my mind to the danger signals. Then on our wedding night it all came to a head when I tripped going up the stairs...'

'I remember!' Jordan laughed reminiscently. 'You stumbled over the hem of your dress and I caught you. And once I had you in my arms—where I had dreamed of having you for months, I might add—I had no intention of letting you go!'

'Jordan! But you were always so...so proper!' Katherine was stunned by the admission. 'You never let me think by a word or a gesture that was how you felt!'

'If I had let you know how I felt, you would have run and not stopped running. I was madly in love with you, Katherine. I fell in love with you the first time your father invited me down to the house for dinner.'

'I had no idea!'

'No, you hadn't.' He kissed her hungrily, then groaned. 'Can't this wait? Who said we should talk right now?'

Katherine felt her heart turn over as she heard the desire which deepened his voice, but she steeled herself.

'We need to clear this up. Then…then I'm at your disposal, Mr James.'

'Promises, promises…' He sighed. 'I knew you had no idea how I felt, although I always sensed your father had guessed. That's why he encouraged our friendship, despite your obvious indifference to me. I told myself that the marriage would work, that I would take things slowly and, if I was lucky, you might grow to feel something for me. And then I blew it within hours of the wedding.'

'You weren't solely to blame. I wanted you in a way I had never dreamt it was possible to want anyone. But it scared me because it simply confirmed all my worst fears. I hadn't married you because I loved you so I felt ashamed that I could respond like that.'

'I loved you, Katherine. You do know that?' He sounded anguished, as though he could hardly bear to hear her say that.

Katherine's eyes filled with tears. 'I don't want to hurt you, but I have to be honest. I didn't marry you for love, but somehow I fell in love with you all the same.'

She felt him stiffen and knew that he was about to say something. She stopped him with a gentle hand on his lips. 'I know it sounds crazy, but it's what I believe. I *was* in love with you, even then, and that's why I wanted you so much on our wedding night, Jordan. It had never been just passion I felt, but I tried to shut what had happened out of my life, to shut *you* out, because I was afraid of how you made me feel. But after you came to Peter's wedding and then you were ill all my defences went tumbling down.'

She frowned as she tilted her head back. 'What made you decide to turn up like that? Was it because Daddy asked you to be there?'

'Partly.' He gave her a rueful grin. 'But mainly because of the old green-eyed monster!' He bent and kissed her, let his lips linger, but his eyes were suddenly serious. 'I kept in contact with your father whenever I was away, Katherine. I know you had no idea because I asked him not to tell you. I think he had the feeling something wasn't quite right, so he was willing to agree because he knew how much I loved you. And it was your father who kept me apprised of your ''friendship'' with Charles Langtree. I put up with it by telling myself I was glad that you had someone to turn to.'

He snorted in disgust. 'Lies! I hated the thought of you and another man! I finally decided enough was enough and came home. Frankly, Katherine, the only man I wanted in your life was me! Langtree was lucky to walk out of his office that day. I would have much preferred to drop him out of the window!'

Katherine laughed softly. 'Jordan…really! And after we owe Charles such a debt of gratitude. I mean, if you hadn't been jealous then you might never have come back.' She paused to twine a wiry coil of black hair around her finger, then gave it a sharp tug. 'Just as if Charles hadn't come to the flat earlier tonight then you might still be in your club, settling down with a cup of cocoa rather than me.'

'Come to the flat…?' Jordan moved so fast that she gasped as he rolled her flat on her back and loomed over her. His eyes glittered with anger; his beautiful mouth was a tight line which told its own tale. 'Did that bastard have the nerve to come here? What did he do? If he laid his hands on you…'

He took a deep breath. Katherine reached up and traced the frown lines between his brows with her fingernail. 'Now, now, Jordan, calm down. You'll wear yourself out like that, and we don't want you getting too tired yet awhile.'

His face softened, but he still felt tense as she slid her hands down to his shoulders. 'What happened, Katherine? I want to know.'

She gave a little shrug, feeling her nipples harden as her breasts brushed against the wall of his chest. Desire uncurled inside her, hot and sweet as wine, and she knew that Jordan had felt her response. 'Charles came here on the pretext of apologising for what happened in the office, but he didn't stay long. He seems to have a similar opinion of you as you have of him—or at least he uses the same descriptive terms. I didn't like it and told him what I thought—how you are twice the man he will ever be.'

She shrugged again, and felt the shudder which rippled through him as her body brushed his. 'I was so angry by then that I decided enough was enough and that it was about time you and I talked. And the rest, as they say, is history.'

Jordan kissed her gently. 'You're not sorry that you came to the club tonight, Katherine?'

She looked him straight in the eye. 'No. I came because I love you, Jordan. I came because you are the most important thing in my life, and it has nothing to do with money or anything else. Peter is getting his life together, my father is happy; now it's up to me to take what I want from life, and that's you. If you'll still have me, of course.'

'Until I die, Katherine, and even beyond. I shall always want you. The last few weeks have been a nightmare.'

'For me too.'

'Darling!'

His kiss was everything she could have dreamt of, but it was far too short. Katherine sat up in alarm as Jordan suddenly shot to his feet. 'What's wrong?'

He strode to the door, grimacing as he glanced at his watch. 'Only that I'm supposed to catch the early flight to Tokyo, and there is no way I'm going by myself!' His eyes adored her. 'How long will it take you to pack?'

Katherine laughed softly. 'About ten minutes, which means we have the rest of the night to spend on other things. Don't be long, darling. It's a shame to waste a second wedding night!'

He gave her a brilliant smile, then disappeared along the hall. Katherine heard him speaking on the phone as she lay back against the pillows.

'Yes, make that two seats now. First class, of course. The name on the other ticket? Katherine James.' He paused before adding softly, 'My wife.'

Katherine closed her eyes and knew that was all she wanted to be from now on—Jordan's wife. Oh, and the mother of his children, of course!

Perfect!

MILLS & BOON®

Next Month's Romances

Each month you can choose from a wide variety of romance novels from Mills & Boon. Below are the new titles to look out for next month from the Presents™ and Enchanted™ series.

Presents™

MISSION: MAKE-OVER	Penny Jordan
BRIDE REQUIRED	Alison Fraser
UP CLOSE AND PERSONAL!	Sandra Field
RELUCTANT FATHER!	Elizabeth Oldfield
THE VALENTINE AFFAIR!	Mary Lyons
A NANNY IN THE FAMILY	Catherine Spencer
TRIAL BY SEDUCTION	Kathleen O'Brien
HIS TEMPORARY MISTRESS	Emma Richmond

Enchanted™

A RUMOURED ENGAGEMENT	Catherine George
BEAUTY AND THE BOSS	Lucy Gordon
THE PERFECT DIVORCE!	Leigh Michaels
BORROWED—ONE BRIDE	Trisha David
SWEET VALENTINE	Val Daniels
KISSING CARLA	Stephanie Howard
MARRY ME	Heather Allison
A HUSBAND MADE IN TEXAS	Rosemary Carter

H1 9801

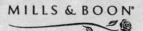

Karen Young

SUGAR BABY

She would do anything to protect her child

Little Danny Woodson's life is threatened when
he witnesses a murder—and only his estranged
uncle can protect him.

"Karen Young is a spellbinding storyteller."

—Publishers Weekly

4 FREE

books and a surprise gift!

We would like to take this opportunity to thank you for reading this Mills & Boon® book by offering you the chance to take FOUR more specially selected titles from the Enchanted™ series absolutely FREE! We're also making this offer to introduce you to the benefits of the Reader Service™—

- ★ FREE home delivery
- ★ FREE gifts and competitions
- ★ FREE monthly newsletter
- ★ Books available before they're in the shops
- ★ Exclusive Reader Service discounts

Accepting these FREE books and gift places you under no obligation to buy, you may cancel at any time, even after receiving your free shipment. Simply complete your details below and return the entire page to the address below. *You don't even need a stamp!*

YES! Please send me 4 free Enchanted books and a surprise gift. I understand that unless you hear from me, I will receive 6 superb new titles every month for just £2.20 each, postage and packing free. I am under no obligation to purchase any books and may cancel my subscription at any time. The free books and gift will be mine to keep in any case.

N8XE

Ms/Mrs/Miss/Mr....................................Initials ....
BLOCK CAPITALS PLEASE

Surname ....

Address ....

....

....Postcode..................................

Send this whole page to:
THE READER SERVICE, FREEPOST, CROYDON, CR9 3WZ
(Eire readers please send coupon to: P.O. BOX 4546, DUBLIN 24.)